THE KINGFISHER TREASURY OF

Dinosaur Stories

CHOSEN BY JEREMY STRONG

ILLUSTRATED BY CLIVE SCRUTON

KINGFISHER

CONTENTS

DINOSAUR SCHOOL

Dick King-Smith

Little Basil Brontosaurus came home from his first morning at playschool in floods of tears.

"Whatever's the matter, darling?" said his mother, whose name was Araminta. "Why are you crying?"

"They've been teasing me," sobbed Basil.

"Who have? The other children?"

A variety of little dinosaurs went to the playschool. There were diplodocuses, iguanodons, ankylosauruses and many others. Basil was the only young brontosaurus.

"Yes," sniffed Basil. "They said I was stupid. They said I hadn't got a brain in my head."

At this point Basil's father, a forty-tonne brontosaurus who measured twenty-seven metres from nose to tail-tip, came lumbering up through the shallows of the lake in which the family lived.

"Herb!" called Araminta. "Did you hear that?

The kids at playschool said our Basil hadn't a brain in his head."

Herb considered this while pulling up and swallowing large amounts of waterweed.

"He has," he said at last. "Hasn't he?"

"Of course you have, darling," said Araminta to her little son. "Come along with me now, and dry your tears and listen carefully."

Still snivelling, Basil waded into the lake. He followed his mother to a quiet spot, well away from the other dinosaurs that were feeding around the shallows.

Araminta settled herself where the water was deep enough to help support her enormous bulk.

"Now listen to Mummy, Basil darling," she said. "What I'm about to tell you is a secret. Every brontosaurus that ever hatched is told this secret by his or her mummy or daddy, once he or she is old enough. One day you'll be grown up, and you'll have a wife of your own, and she'll lay eggs, and then you'll have babies. And when those babies are old enough, they'll have to be told, just like I'm going to tell you."

"Tell me what?" said Basil.

"Promise not to breathe word of it to the other children?"

"All right. But what is it?"

"It is this," said Araminta. "We have two brains."

"You're joking," said Basil.

"I'm not. Every brontosaurus has two brains. One in its head and one in the middle of its back."

"Wow!" cried Basil. "Well, if I've got two brains and all the other kids have only got one, I must be twice as clever as them."

"You are, darling," said Araminta. "You are. So let's have no more of this cry-baby nonsense. Next time one of the children teases you, just think to yourself, 'I am twice as clever as you.'"

Not only did Basil think this, next morning at playschool, but he also thought that he was twice as big as the other children.

"Did you have a nice time?" said Araminta, when he came home.

"Smashing," said Basil.

"No tears?"

"Not mine," said Basil cheerily.

"You didn't tell anyone our secret?"

"Oh no," said Basil. "I didn't do much talking to the other kids. Actions speak louder than words."

Not long after this the playschool teacher, an elderly female stegosaurus, came to see Herb and Araminta.

"I'm sorry to bother you," she said, "but I'm a little worried about Basil."

"Not been blubbing again, has he?" said Herb.

10

"Oh no, *he* hasn't," said the stegosaurus. "In fact, recently he has grown greatly in confidence. At first he was rather nervous and the other children tended to make fun of him, but they don't any more. He's twice the boy he was."

"Can't think why," said Herb, but Araminta could.

"Indeed," the stegosaurus went on, "I fear that lately he's been throwing his weight about. Boys will be boys, I know, but really Basil has become very rough. Only yesterday I had to send home a baby brachiosaurus with a badly bruised foot and a little trachodon with a black eye. I should be glad if you would speak to Basil about all this."

When the teacher had departed, Araminta said to Herb, "You must have a word with the boy."

"Why?" said Herb.

"You heard what the teacher said. He's been bullying the other children. He's obviously getting above himself."

At this point Basil appeared.

"What did old Steggy want?" he said.

"Tell him, Herb," said Araminta.

"Now look here, my boy," said Herb.

Basil looked.

"You listen to me."

Basil listened, but Herb, Araminta could see, had forgotten what he was talking about.

"Your father is very angry with you," she said. "You have been fighting. At playschool."

"That's right," said Herb. "Fighting. At playschool. Why?"

"Well, it's like this, Dad," said Basil. "The first day, the other kids teased me. They said I hadn't got a brain in my head, remember? And then Mum told me I had. And another in the middle of my back. Two brains! So I thought: I'm twice as clever as the rest as well as twice as big, so why not lean on them a bit? Not my fault if they get under my feet."

"You want to watch your step," said Herb.

"Daddy's right," said Araminta. "One of these days you'll get into real trouble. Now run along, I want to talk to your father."

"It's all my fault for telling him about having two brains," she said when Basil had gone. "He's too young. My parents didn't tell me till I was nearly grown up. How did you find out?"

"Oh, I don't know," said Herb. "I dare say I heard some of the chaps talking down in the swamp. When I was one of the gang. We used to talk a lot, down in the swamp."

"What about?" said Araminta.

"Waterweed, mostly," said Herb, and he pulled up a great mouthful and began to chomp.

Not long after this, Basil was expelled.

"I'm sorry," said the elderly stegosaurus, "but I can't have the boy in my class any longer. It isn't only his roughness, it's his rudeness. Do you know what he said to me today?"

"No," said Herb.

"What?" said Araminta.

"He said to me, 'I'm twice as clever as you are.'"

"Is he?" said Herb.

"Of course he isn't," said Araminta hastily. "He was just being silly and childish. I'm sure he won't be any trouble in the future."

"Not in my playschool he won't," said the steogsaurus and then, oddly, she used the very words that Araminta had used earlier.

"One of these days," she said, "he'll get into real trouble." And off she waddled, flapping her back plates angrily.

And one of those days, Basil did. Being expelled from playschool hadn't worried him at all. What do I want with other dinosaurs? he thought. I'm far superior to them, with my two brains, one to work my neck and my front legs, one to work my back legs and my tail. Brontosauruses are twice as clever as other dinosaurs and I'm twice as clever as any other brontosaurus.

You couldn't say that Basil was big-headed, for that was almost the smallest part of him, but you could certainly say that he was boastful, conceited and arrogant.

"That boy!" said Araminta to Herb. "He's boastful, conceited and arrogant. He must get it from your side of the family, swaggering about and picking fights all the time. What does he think he is? A *Tyrannosaurus rex*?"

"What do you think you are?" Basil was saying at that very moment. He had come out of the lake where the family spent almost all their time, and set off for a walk.

He was ambling along, thinking what a fine fellow he was, when suddenly he saw a strange, smallish dinosaur standing in his path.

It was not like any dinosaur he had ever seen before. It stood upright on its hind legs, which

14

were much bigger than its little forelegs, and it had a large head with large jaws and a great many teeth. But compared to Basil, who already weighed a couple of tonnes, it looked quite small, and he advanced upon it, saying in a rude tone, "What do you think you are?"

"I'm a *Tyrannosaurus rex*," said the stranger.

"Never heard of you," said Basil.

"Lucky you."

"Why? What's so wonderful about you? You can't even walk on four feet like a decent dinosaur and you've only got one brain. You'll be telling me next that you don't eat waterweed like we do."

"We don't," said the other. "We only eat meat."

"What sort of meat?"

"Brontosaurus, mostly."

"Let's get this straight," said Basil. "Are you seriously telling me that you kill brontosauruses and eat them?"

"Yes."

"Don't make me laugh," said Basil. "I'm four times as big as you."

"Yes," said the youngster, "but my dad's four times as big as you. Oh, look, what a bit of luck. Here he comes!"

Basil looked up to see a terrifying sight.

Marching towards him on its huge hind legs was a towering, full-grown *Tyrannosaurus rex* with a mouthful of long razor-sharp teeth. All of a sudden Basil had two brainwaves.

Time I went, he thought. Sharpish. And as one brain sent a message rippling along to the other, he turned tail and made for the safety of the lake as fast as his legs could carry him. This was not very fast, as Basil's big body made him slow and clumsy on land. If the tyrannosaurus had been really hungry, he would have caught Basil without any trouble.

As it was, Basil reached the shore of the lake just in time and splashed frantically out to deeper water, where his parents, their long necks outstretched, were browsing on the weedy bottom.

Araminta was the first to look up.

"Hello, darling," she said. "Where have you been? Whatever's the matter? You're all of a doodah."

"Oh, Mummy, Mummy!" panted Basil. "It was awful! I went for a walk and I was nearly eaten by a *Tyrannosaurus rex*!"

Herb raised his head in time to hear this.

"That'll teach you," he said.

"Teach me what, Dad?"

"Not to be so cocky," said Araminta. "Ever since I told you that secret you've been unbearable, Basil. I hope this will be a lesson to you."

"Oh, it will, Mummy, it will!" cried Basil. "I won't ever shoot my mouth off again."

"And don't go for walks," said his mother, "but keep close to the lake, where you'll be safe from the tyrannosaurus."

"In case he rex you," said Herb, and plunged his head under water again, while strings of bubbles rose as he laughed at his own joke.

"And if you want to grow up to be as big as your father," said Araminta, "there's one thing you must always remember to do."

"What's that, Mummy?" said Basil.

"Use your brains."

THE STRANGE EGG

Margaret Mahy

Once Molly found a strange leathery egg in the swamp. She put it under Mrs Warm the broody hen to hatch it out. It hatched out into a sort of dragon.

Her father said, "This is no ordinary dragon. This is a dinosaur."

"What is a dinosaur?" asked Molly.

"Well," said her father, "a long time ago there were a lot of dinosaurs. They were all big lizards. Some of them were bigger than houses. They all died long ago ... All except this one," he added gloomily. "I hope it is not one of the larger meat-eating lizards as then it might grow up to worry the sheep."

The dinosaur followed Mrs Warm about. She scratched worms for it, but the dinosaur liked plants better.

"Ah," said Molly's father. "It is a plant-eating

dinosaur – one of the milder kind. They are stupid but good-natured," he added.

Professors of all ages came from near and far to see Molly's dinosaur. She led it around on a string. Every day she needed a longer piece of string. The dinosaur grew as big as ten elephants. It ate all the flowers in the garden and Molly's mother got cross.

"I am tired of having no garden and I am tired of making tea for all the professors," she said. "Let's send the dinosaur to the zoo."

"No," said Father. "The place wouldn't be the same without it."

So the dinosaur stayed. Mrs Warm used to perch on it every night. She had never before hatched such a grand successful egg.

One day it began to rain . . . It rained and rained and rained and rained so heavily that the water in the river got deep and overflowed.

"A flood, a flood – we will drown," screamed Molly's mother.

"Hush, dear," said Molly's father. "We will ride to a safe place on Molly's dinosaur. Whistle to him, Molly."

Molly whistled and the dinosaur came towards her with Mrs Warm the hen, wet and miserable, on his back. Molly and her father and mother climbed on to the dinosaur's back with her. They held an umbrella over themselves and had warm drinks out of a thermos flask. Just as they left, the house was swept away by the flood.

"Well, dear, there you are," said Molly's father. "You see it was useful to have a dinosaur, after all. And I am now able to tell you that this is the biggest kind of dinosaur and its name is Brontosaurus."

Molly was pleased to think her pet had such a long, dignified-sounding name. It matched him well. As they went along they rescued a lot of other people climbing trees and house tops, and floating on chicken crates and fruit boxes. They rescued cats and dogs, two horses and an elephant which was floating away from a circus. The dinosaur paddled on cheerfully. By the time they came in sight of dry land,

his back was quite crowded. On the land policemen were getting boats ready to go looking for people, but all the people were safe on the dinosaur's back.

After the flood went down and everything was as it should be, a fine medal was given to Molly's dinosaur as most heroic animal of the year and many presents were given to him.

The biggest present of all was a great big swimming-pool made of rubber so you could blow it up. It was so big it took one man nearly a year to blow it up. It was a good size for dinosaurs of the brontosaurus type. He lived in the swimming-pool after that (and Molly's mother was able to grow her flowers again). It is well known that brontosauruses like to swim and paddle. It took the weight off his feet. Mrs Warm the hen used to swim with him a bit, and it is not very often you find a swimming hen.

So you see this story has a happy ending after all, which is not easy with a pet as big as ten elephants. And just to end the story I must tell you that though Molly's dinosaur had the long name of Brontosaurus, Molly always called it "Rosie".

DINOSAURS AT THE SUPERMARKET

Lindsay Camp

Once there was a little girl called Laura whose best friend was a crocodile. He wasn't a very big crocodile or very fierce. In fact, he was rather shy, and liked being tickled. His name was Brigadier Simpson.

Laura's father couldn't see Brigadier Simpson. Actually, nobody could, and people were always stepping on his tail and sitting on him.

One day, Laura and Brigadier Simpson were in the garden, digging for buried treasure. They found a stone with a swirly round pattern on it. Laura took it inside to her father.

"It's a fossil," he said.

"What's a fossil?" asked Laura.

"Well," answered her father, "it's difficult to explain. It's sort of what's left of the bones of creatures who died out millions of years ago, long before there were even any people on earth."

"Like dinosaurs, you mean?"

"Mmm," said Laura's father, turning back to his computer. "Something like that . . ."

Laura was very excited and hurried back to Brigadier Simpson. "Daddy says it's a dinosaur bone! It's called a . . . I can't remember what it's called. But it's definitely a dinosaur bone. The dinosaur must have lived in our garden!"

She looked around doubtfully.

The garden wasn't very big.

There was barely room for the jungle gym. Still, Brigadier Simpson was looking very nervous.

"Don't worry," said Laura. "He's not here anymore. Daddy said all the dinosaurs died out millions of years ago."

That night, Laura slept with the dinosaur bone under her pillow. The next day, she carried it everywhere. She even carried it into her bath, where she had a scary thought. What if the dinosaur wasn't really dead? What if he wanted his bone back? She didn't say anything to Brigadier Simpson, because she didn't want to frighten him.

Later, when her father finished reading her bedtime story, she asked him if he was really sure about all the dinosaurs being dead.

"Very sure," said her father. "Now, go to sleep."

When Laura looked out the window in the morning, there was a dinosaur. He tried to hide behind the shed where the lawnmower lived, but he wasn't quick enough. Laura had seen him.

Laura got out her dinosaur book. There, on the front, was the same dinosaur.

Laura asked her father what the dinosaur on the book was called. He said it was a *Tyrannosaurus rex*, and it was definitely dead.

But Laura knew he was wrong.

Later, Laura saw the dinosaur again. This time, he didn't hide. And this time, he wasn't alone.

He was with his friends, and they were whispering together. Laura knew they were talking about how to get the bone back.

Laura wondered what to do.

If she gave the bone back, the dinosaurs might go away. But she didn't want to give it back. It was her treasure. And she was sure the dinosaur could manage without one tiny bone.

Laura decided to keep the bone. She still took it everywhere. But now the dinosaurs followed.

She saw them outside the supermarket. They had put their huge feet in the shopping carts and were whizzing around as if they were on roller skates.

She saw them at the library. They were stamping and roaring so loudly that it was difficult for Laura to choose her book.

When she went to school the next day, they were waiting in the playground. All day long they took turns peering at her through the classroom window.

But the funny thing was, the dinosaurs didn't do anything to Laura. They didn't chase her. They didn't jump out at her when she wasn't expecting it. And they didn't try to catch Brigadier Simpson and hold him prisoner until Laura gave back the bone.

They just followed her. Everywhere.

Then one day Laura's class went on a trip to the museum. The dinosaurs came too. They seemed to like it at the museum.

Upstairs, there were big rooms full of glass cases with old things inside. CLACK, CLACK, CLACK went Laura's shoes on the shiny floor. CLUMP, CLUMP, CLUMP went the dinosaurs' feet.

Suddenly, Laura stopped and stared. There, in a glass case right in front of her, was a dinosaur bone exactly like hers! It was a lot bigger, but it was definitely a bone from the same dinosaur.

Laura looked back at the dinosaurs. They seemed angry, showing their teeth and pushing into the room. Softly she asked the museum lady about the bone.

"It's called an ammonite," she said, "and when it was alive it was a little creature, like a snail, that lived under the sea."

Laura couldn't believe her ears. A snail! But hadn't Daddy said it was a dinosaur bone? And if it wasn't, why were the dinosaurs following her?

Laura turned around quickly. The dinosaurs were gone.

Laura thought that the dinosaurs might be waiting in the playground back at school. But they weren't.

And they weren't in the garden when she got home, either. They'd definitely disappeared.

That night, Laura felt very sad. When her father finished reading her story, he saw she was crying.

"What's the matter?" he asked.

"You remember that dinosaur bone I found in the garden? I'm sure you said it was a dinosaur bone, but it wasn't. It was just a snail! The lady in the museum told me."

Laura's father hugged her, and said, "I'm sorry. It was my fault – I was busy and I didn't explain properly when you showed it to me."

"That's all right, Daddy," said Laura. She still felt sad but she stopped crying when Daddy kissed her goodnight.

Brigadier Simpson, who didn't want Daddy to sit on him, waited until Daddy left before snuggling into bed with Laura. Soon they were both fast asleep.

The next morning, Laura felt better. The sun was shining and Brigadier Simpson was already bouncing around.

Laura looked at him. There was something different about him. She closed her eyes, then looked again.

There was no doubt about it. Something had happened to Brigadier Simpson in the night. He wasn't a crocodile anymore – he was a dinosaur, just like the first one that Laura had seen in her garden!

Laura jumped happily out of bed. "Come on," she said. "We'd better hurry, or we'll be late for school."

DILLY'S PET

Tony Bradman

"Father, can I have a pet?" asked Dilly one day.
"What, Dilly?" said Father.

It was a lovely, sunny morning, and we were all in the garden. Mother was basking in the sunshine, I was reading, Father was doing some gardening, and Dilly was supposed to be playing. But he was following Father around being a pest instead.

"All my friends have got pets," said Dilly. "I'm the only one who hasn't."

Dilly had caught up with Father in the part of the garden where the swamp roses grow. They're Father's favourite flowers, and he spends ages looking after them.

Father's always telling us about the little creatures which come into the garden to eat his plants. He says there's one in particular which just loves swamp roses. It's called a swamp lizard, and if we ever find one in the garden, we're supposed to tell him.

"I'm sorry, Dilly," he said, "but your mother and I don't think you're ready to have a pet just yet."

"But I *am* ready, Father," said Dilly. "I've been ready for ages!"

"What I mean, Dilly," said Father with a sigh, "is that you're not old enough yet. Pets can be hard work. You have to make them somewhere to live, remember to feed them regularly and maybe even take them for walks. We think you'd probably forget to do all that."

"But I wouldn't, Father!" said Dilly. "I *promise* I wouldn't!"

"I'm sorry, Dilly," said Father. "The answer is still no. You'll just have to wait until you're older."

"It's not fair!" shouted Dilly. "I want a pet and

I'm going to have one!" He stamped his foot, and swished his tail around, and for a second I thought he was going to have a tantrum. Father was beginning to look angry, too. Luckily, Mother came to the rescue.

"It's such a lovely day," she said quickly. "Why don't we all go swamp wallowing?"

Dilly soon changed his tune. He loves swamp wallowing, and he couldn't wait to go. But if Mother and Father thought he'd forgotten about having a pet, they were wrong, as we found out later . . .

The next morning, I went with Father to the Shopping Cavern to buy a new pair of shoes for school. When we got home, Mother was cooking lunch and Dilly was playing in the garden. I took the lid off the box and showed Mother my new shoes.

"They're perfect, Dorla," she said. "Why don't you show them to Dilly? You can tell him his toasted fern stalks are ready, too."

I went into the garden, and at first I couldn't see Dilly. Then I saw his tail sticking out from behind the giant fern. He seemed to be kneeling down and looking at something on the ground. I couldn't see what it was.

"What *are* you doing, Dilly?" I said. Dilly jumped and looked round at me. He stood up, but I noticed that he kept both paws behind his back.

"Nothing," he said. I didn't believe him, though. He had his I-Know-I'm-Doing-Something-Wrong-But-I-Don't-Care look on his face.

I told him that lunch was ready, and showed him my new shoes in the box. I thought he'd say "Yuck!" or "They're stupid!" like he usually does, but he didn't. In fact he didn't really look at them. He was interested in something else.

"Can I have the box?" he said. "*Please*, Dorla?"

I was so surprised he'd said "please" that I took the shoes out and gave him the box right there and then. We went back into the house, and Dilly ran upstairs.

"Dilly!" called Mother. "Where are you going? Your lunch is on the table!"

"Coming, Mother," Dilly called out. He came back downstairs and sat at the table. He didn't have the shoe box with him.

Dilly was very quiet and well behaved at lunch. As you know, he usually makes a real mess with his food, and he often spills his pineapple juice. But today he didn't do any of that, although he *was* rather slow. In fact, when everyone else had finished, Dilly's plate looked as if he'd hardly started.

Father told him he'd have to hurry up and finish while the rest of us tidied our dishes away.

"I will, Father," said Dilly. And he did, too. The moment Mother, Father and I went out of the dining room and into the kitchen, he must have speeded up a lot. For when we came back, Dilly's plate was completely empty, and he was sitting there with a big smile on his face.

"Well, Dilly," said Father. He looked rather surprised. "You must have been hungry after all."

Dilly went up to his room after that, but he didn't stay in there for very long. After a while, there was a knock on my door. I opened it, and Dilly was standing there. He gave me a big smile.

"Can I *please* borrow some of your doll's house furniture, Dorla?" he asked, very politely. "I promise I won't break it."

Usually I won't let Dilly near my doll's house. But he'd asked so nicely, I couldn't really say no, especially as I could see Mother standing on the stairs listening. I let him choose what he wanted, and then he went back to his room.

Mother said it was nice to see Dilly being well behaved for a change. I didn't say anything.

That's because I was sure he was up to something.

I was even more sure of it later when he did something very strange. He came downstairs with the shoe box and asked Mother if he could go into the garden. She said he could. He went outside, marched round the garden twice, came back inside, and went straight up to his room. He looked really happy.

I kept my eye on Dilly all evening, but I couldn't work out what he was doing.

The next day, Dilly asked Mother if he could go into the garden again. He had the shoe box with him, and he kept looking at it. He seemed a little worried.

"Of course you can, Dilly," said Mother. Dilly hurried outside, and I didn't think any more about it.

A little later, Father said he was going to do some gardening. He hadn't been outside long when we heard him call out. Mother and I went into the garden. Father was standing in the part where the swamp roses grow. He looked rather upset.

"They're gone," he said. "Every last one of them!"

It was true. The stalks had been stripped bare. Then I noticed a petal lying on the ground, and another, and another . . . They made a trail which led us to the giant fern. We went round behind it, and there was Dilly with his shoe box.

"Dilly," said Father, "I think you'd better show me what's in the box."

Dilly didn't say anything. He just stopped smiling and held on to the box more tightly.

"Come on, Dilly," said Father. "Hand it over."

Dilly didn't hand it over. Instead, he blasted our ears with an ultra-special, 150-mile-per-hour super-scream, the sort that sends us all diving for cover behind the nearest fern bush.

We soon discovered what it was all about once Dilly had calmed down. Inside the shoe box was a swamp lizard he had found and made into his pet. He'd wanted my shoe box and doll's house furniture

to make it a home, and all that marching round the garden had been to give his pet a walk.

He hadn't eaten his lunch the day before, either. He'd slipped it into a pocket for his pet when we weren't looking. The lizard had drunk some pineapple juice, but hadn't touched any of the toasted fern stalks. Dilly had been worried he would starve. Then he'd remembered that there was a flower swamp lizards just loved to eat . . .

Of course, Father was very cross. Dilly was told off and sent to his room for the rest of the day.

Later, at bedtime, I heard Dilly say he was sorry. He also asked Father if he could keep the swamp lizard.

"I did all the things you said, Father. So I must be ready to have a pet."

"I'll think about it," said Father. Then he sighed. "*You* might be ready, Dilly – but I'm not sure if *I* am yet . . ."

THE LITTLEST
DINOSAUR

Terrance Dicks

"'Tis!" shouted Elly.

"'Tisn't!" yelled Olly.

"Quiet, you two!" called their mother.

They were in Mr Orlovsky's antique shop: a long, thin, amazingly untidy room full of – well, it was full of old junk really, but Mr Orlovsky liked to call it antiques. Mrs Elkins, Olly and Elly's mother, was looking at a coffee table.

"Genuine Georgian," said Mr Orlovsky. "A bargain at ten pounds!"

Mrs Elkins sniffed. "Genuine junk, more like it. Might be worth five ..."

They were just settling down for a good haggle when they were interrupted by the fuss from the back of the shop. The twins, Oliver and Eleanor, Olly and Elly for short, were arguing again. They'd started fighting as babies in their big twin pram, and had kept it up ever since.

Mrs Elkins sighed. "What are you two fighting about now?" she asked.

"It's this egg," said Elly.

"It's not an egg," said Olly. "Not a real one anyway."

"'Tis!"

"'Tisn't!"

"Don't start that again!" said their mother. "Bring the thing here and let's have a look at it."

Olly and Elly came forward from the gloom at the back of the shop. Elly was clutching something that certainly looked like an enormous egg. It was very big and a sort of dingy yellow in colour. "We found it in an old chest," explained Elly. "I think it's an ostrich egg."

"Rubbish," said Olly. "It's made of plaster."

"'Tisn't!"

"'Tis!"

"Hush!" said Mrs Elkins. She turned to Mr Orlovsky. "Well?"

Mr Orlovsky was small and tubby, with a shining bald head that looked very much like an egg itself. "To be honest, I'm not sure . . . But that chest came from the house of a famous explorer. He travelled all over the world: Africa, China, the North Pole . . ."

Mrs Elkins took the strange object from Elly's hands. It had a rough, leathery feel. "Well, it's certainly not marble or anything like that."

"Can we have it, Mum?" asked Elly eagerly.

Mr Orlovsky seized his chance. "I tell you what. For a favourite customer, with such charming children . . . You give me eight pounds for the table and I throw in the egg for free!"

"Seven!" said Mrs Elkins.

"Seven-fifty?"

"Done!"

"Well," said Olly. "What are you going to do with it?"

They were sitting in the garden, the egg on the grass between them.

"Hatch it!" said Elly firmly.

"What are you going to do — sit on it?" Olly jumped up and down making chicken noises. "You'll look a real twit, perched on a plaster egg!"

"Don't be so silly, Olly. We'll hatch it in Dad's greenhouse!"

Picking up the egg, Elly led the way down the garden and into the greenhouse. The air felt hot and damp and steamy, just like a jungle. They found a big empty plant-pot and put the egg inside, covering it with peat. Then Elly put the pot under a bench, hiding it with a sack.

"We'll come in and check on it every day, when no one's about."

The first time they checked, the egg hadn't changed at all, except for being a bit warmer.

"See?" said Olly.

"*Wait* and see!" said Elly.

On the second day the egg was covered with a network of fine cracks. It felt hotter, and it seemed to be throbbing ...

"Well?" said Elly triumphantly.

For once, Olly was speechless.

On the third day there were even more cracks.

 The egg was shaking, and it seemed to be bulging from the inside.

Suddenly the shell cracked open, and a blunt little head popped out. It looked at Elly, and then at Olly.

"Eek!" it said. "Eek!"

Struggling wildly, the little creature kicked itself free of the shell.

It had powerful back legs, a long tail, and tiny arms and hands dangling in front of it.

"That's no ostrich," said Olly.

"I know," said Elly. "It's a baby dinosaur!"

The tiny dinosaur looked up at them with bright little eyes. It peered into their faces, looking first at Elly, then at Olly.

"It's imprinting," whispered Elly. "I saw it on one of those nature programmes. When chicks come out of the shell, they think the first thing they see is their mum. Maybe it works for dinosaurs too!"

"So it thinks we're its mum and dad?"

"That's right."

"Eek!" said the little dinosaur. "Eek! Eek! Eek!"

Its wide open mouth reminded Elly of something else she'd seen on a nature programme – little birds in a nest waiting to be fed.

"I think it's hungry. What do dinosaurs eat?"

Olly scratched his head. "Other dinosaurs?"

"Not to start with, surely …" Elly looked round the greenhouse. She went over to a tomato plant and picked a ripe and juicy tomato. "Lend me your penknife, Olly."

She cut the tomato up into little pieces and dropped one into the baby dinosaur's mouth. It gulped it down, looked pleased and said "Eek!" once more. Elly dropped another bit of tomato into the gaping mouth. Then another and another …

When the whole tomato was gone, the dinosaur burped happily. Then it rolled over on its back and went to sleep.

Olly looked down at it. "Are you sure it's a dinosaur? It's the littlest dinosaur I've ever seen!"

"That's what we'll call it," said Elly. "We'll call it Littlest!"

"Never mind what we call it, what do we *do* with it? If we leave it here, it'll scoff all Dad's tomatoes."

"Or it might just wake up and run off," said Elly. "We'll have to smuggle it into the house!"

They put the sleeping Littlest in a cardboard box, covered him with a bit of sacking and carried him up to Elly's room.

For the next few days, Littlest lived perfectly happily in the blanket-lined bottom shelf of Elly's toy-cupboard. Olly and Elly spent as much time with him as they could. Their mother was always telling them to eat more fruit, and she was pleased to see that they seemed to be taking notice at last. She didn't realize that the fruit was disappearing into Olly and Elly's pockets – and soon afterwards into Littlest's tummy.

Littlest ate and ate – and grew and grew. Before very long, he'd grown from the size of a chick to that of a chicken.

"This can't go on, you know," said Olly one day.

They were watching Littlest playing with a ball from the toy-cupboard. It was one of those baby balls with a little bell inside. Littlest loved it. He

spent ages kicking it up and down the room with his powerful back legs.

"The only footballing dinosaur in captivity!" said Elly proudly. "What can't go on?"

"Keeping a pet dinosaur hidden in your bedroom. Look how much it's grown."

Elly rolled the ball away so Littlest could chase it. "So?"

"Well, it'll go on growing, won't it? Growing and growing . . . It'll get too big for the toy-cupboard, too big for the room. It'll burst out and go stomping around London smashing down houses. You'll catch it then – Mum will be furious!"

"You've been watching too many monster movies on TV," said Elly.

"And how long is it going to be satisfied with just fruit?" went on Olly. "Any day now it'll start craving meat. And you know what the nearest meat is? Us!"

Olly was going over the top as usual, thought Elly. But perhaps there was *something* in what he was saying.

"We do need to know more about dinosaurs," she agreed. "What they eat, how fast they grow, everything ..."

"We could try the library," said Olly.

Elly shook her head. "I've got a better idea. There's a special dinosaur exhibition at the Natural History Museum. We'll go and visit it. Once we know what kind of dinosaur Littlest is, we can decide what to do."

"Eek!" said a little voice from Elly's school bag.

"Shut up!" hissed Olly.

Olly and Elly were at the Natural History Museum, waiting in line to enter the dinosaur exhibition. They hadn't intended to bring Littlest as well, but when they tried to leave him behind the little dinosaur had made the most tremendous fuss, shrieking "Eek! Eek! Eek!" and scrabbling against the door.

Eventually they'd been forced to give in and bring Littlest with them, tucked into Elly's school bag.

"We'll have had it if anyone finds out Littlest is here in the Museum," whispered Olly.

"I don't see why," said Elly. "What's wrong with bringing a dinosaur to a dinosaur exhibition?"

They moved on through the huge hall. There were illuminated display cases and notice boards, models and skeletons, pictures of dinosaurs of every kind – but none that looked quite like Littlest.

There was even a model dinosaur's nest with lots of baby dinosaurs popping out of eggs.

The high spot of the exhibition was a life-size tableau. You went up some stairs and looked down from a walkway.

Down below, in a rocky prehistoric landscape, a huge dead dinosaur was being eaten by three smaller ones. Their claws and teeth were red, and they made harsh croaking sounds.

Littlest popped his head out of the bag for a look, gave a horrified "Eek!" and popped back inside.

Olly gave Elly a nudge. "See?"

Elly shuddered. Was Littlest really going to turn into a rampaging monster?

They came out of the exhibition and stopped for tea and buns in a little café area in the main hall of the museum.

A muffled "Eek!" came from the bag. Elly bought an orange, popping segments into the school bag to keep Littlest quiet.

"I've got so much dinosaur information in my brain it feels like bursting," she said.

Olly nodded. "Me too! Nothing that helps with our problem though."

"We could try the book shop."

"Oh sure! Maybe they've got a copy of 'How to Look After Your Pet Dinosaur'!"

"A fat lot of help you are!" said Elly. "All you can do is make silly jokes."

"Well, if you hadn't hatched that egg in the first place ..."

In no time at all, Olly and Elly were off on one of their famous rows. They were so busy arguing that they didn't notice what was happening in the school bag at Elly's feet.

The orange was all finished and Littlest was getting very bored with being shut up. He wriggled his head out of the bag. Then his long neck – and then the rest of him. Claws clattering on the stone floor, Littlest jumped out of the bag and looked around.

Elly saw what was happening – just too late! She made a grab for Littlest's tail, missing it by inches.

Confused by the chatter of the crowd and the wide open space all around, Littlest panicked.

With a shrill "Eek! Eek! Eek!", the little dinosaur ran away.

The hall was filled with mums and dads and kids who'd come to see the dinosaur exhibition. They hadn't bargained on meeting a real one! There were yells of amazement as Littlest dashed across the big echoing hall.

A dignified-looking lady screamed as Littlest shot between her legs.

An astonished toddler howled and dropped his ice cream as the little dinosaur whizzed by.

An angry old gentleman tried to hook the fleeing Littlest with the handle of his walking stick, but Littlest leaped over the stick and disappeared down a side passage.

Grabbing her bag, Elly chased after him, Olly close behind. They tore down the corridor, past displays of snakes and fishes and lizards, and along a white-walled corridor lined with office doors.

Suddenly they found themselves in another crowded exhibition hall. In the middle of the room there was a life-sized model of a whale, surrounded by elephants and rhinoceroses.

Amidst more shouts and screams, Littlest shot underneath the whale, dodged in and out of the elephants and rhinos, circled right round the hall, and streaked out the way he'd come in.

Olly and Elly panted along behind him, shoving past astonished museum visitors with shouts of "'Scuse me!" and "Sorry!".

Soon they were chasing Littlest back down the white-walled corridor. A group of tourists appeared, blocking the far end.

"Now we've got him!" yelled Olly – but they hadn't.

There was a flight of stone steps on the left, barred by a "No Entry" barrier. Littlest jumped over the barrier and disappeared up the stairs. Ducking under the bar, Olly and Elly followed.

The steps led them to another corridor much like the first. Just ahead they could see Littlest, still sprinting along.

"He's not even tired," gasped Elly.

"I am," said Olly. "And I've got a stitch. We'll never catch him."

Just then a tall, thin man appeared round the corner, ahead of Littlest. He had big glasses and lots of straggly grey hair. He was reading a book as he walked along, and he didn't notice the little

dinosaur – not until he tripped over him! Then he crashed to the ground, falling on top of Littlest who gave an angry "Eek!"

Before Littlest could set off again, Elly ran up and grabbed him.

The tall man picked himself up, blinked and said mildly, "Am I mistaken, or is that a live dinosaur you have there?"

"Well . . ." said Elly.

They heard shouting coming from below – and it was getting nearer. "Maybe we'd better talk in my office," said the tall man.

He led them around the corner, along a smaller corridor and into a tiny cluttered room, filled with books and old bones.

"Now then," he said, closing the door.

"It's like this," said Olly.

"We found this egg," said Elly.

Talking in turn, and sometimes both together, they poured out the whole story.

"Astonishing!" said the tall man. He looked hard at Littlest, who'd jumped down from Elly's lap and was pottering around the room. "But why did you bring the creature here?"

"We needed to know more about dinosaurs," said Elly.

"Like how long we've got before he grows enormous and starts trampling down buildings and eating people," explained Olly.

The tall man chuckled. "I don't think you need worry about that!"

Elly stared at him. "What do you mean?"

"What you have here is an eichinodon, one of the smaller dinosaurs. It won't grow much bigger than it is now. And as for eating people – the eichinodon is a vegetarian."

"Are you sure?" said Olly.

"I happen to be a Professor of Natural History," said the tall man. "Dinosaurs are my special subject – I've been studying them all my life." He tickled Littlest under the chin. "Mind you, this is the first chance I've had to study a live one!"

"Then we can keep him!" said Elly happily.

"What about Mum and Dad?" asked Olly. "We can't keep Littlest a secret much longer."

"Suppose I write to your parents," suggested the Professor. "I'll tell them that by looking after Littlest you'll be helping the Museum with important scientific research."

"Wonderful!" said Elly. "They're dead keen on anything educational."

"What about our chasing Littlest round the Museum?" asked Olly. "Won't there be a huge fuss?"

"I doubt it," said the Professor. "When they see something impossible, people just don't believe their eyes. Pretty soon everyone will be convinced it was a dog or a cat or a chicken."

Soon it was all arranged, and Olly and Elly and Littlest were on their way home. On the bus, Littlest popped his head out of the bag, looking around curiously. Luckily they were upstairs in the front seat and nobody noticed.

"He's going to be quite a handful," said Olly.

"Who cares?" said Elly. "Littlest is the only living dinosaur – and he's ours!"

"Eek!" said Littlest happily. "Eek! Eek! Eek!"

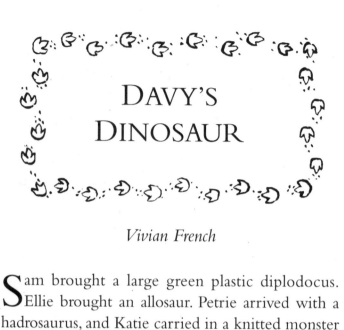

DAVY'S DINOSAUR

Vivian French

Sam brought a large green plastic diplodocus. Ellie brought an allosaur. Petrie arrived with a hadrosaurus, and Katie carried in a knitted monster that she said was a sauropod.

"That's rubbish," Liam said. "The other kids'll laugh at it."

"No they won't." Mrs Frederick was firm. "When we put the final display up in the hall they'll be staggered. Our Dinosaur Day is going to be FANTASTIC!"

Sam and Ian and Davy and Liam made mountains and trees and lakes for the dinosaur landscape. Sam put his diplodocus under a clump of greenery, and Ian balanced his triceratops on a rock. Liam put a brachiosaurus on the mountain with a flourish.

"It should be a tyrannosaurus rex on the top," Sam said. "They were the biggest. And the fiercest."

"Mine's big," Liam said. "It weighed thirty tonnes!"

"Yes, but it ate plants," Sam said. "It wasn't a killer."

"What did you bring, Davy?" Ian asked.

Davy shuffled his feet. He didn't like to admit that he hadn't actually got any dinosaur models at home. Neither did he want to say that he couldn't buy anything because he was still paying Dad back for breaking the kitchen window.

"I'm bringing something later," he said. "Wait and see!"

"Bet you don't," Liam said. "Bet you haven't got anything – you'll have to make one out of plasticine like Suzie and Ben!"

Davy turned his back on Liam. He hated the smell of plasticine, and his models always fell over because he made them too quickly. "I'm bringing something really SPECIAL," he said, and crossed his fingers to make it happen.

The trouble was that it didn't. The days went by, and the display was nearly finished. Everyone in the class had made or found a dinosaur to put on the dinosaur landscape . . . everyone except Davy.

"PLEASE, Mum," he begged. "PLEASE can I buy a tyrannosaurus rex? I'll go on paying Dad back afterwards – promise!"

But Mum shook her head, and Davy sank into despair . . . until the parcel arrived the morning before Dinosaur Day.

"It's for Tim," Mum said as she looked at the label.

"Why's Tim got a parcel?" Davy asked. "His birthday was ages ago."

"It's from Gran," said Dad, "she's always late for birthdays. It's probably socks."

"It's really hard to open," Tim said. "Why's she used so much sticky tape?"

"Here," said Mum. "Use scissors."

Tim hacked his way into the parcel. "Oh," he said. "It's a blow-up dinosaur. Bit babyish."

"Gran forgets," Dad said. "She still thinks you're at primary school."

Davy flew round the table to look. "A DINOSAUR?" His voice was wobbly with excitement. "Is it – is it a T. rex?"

Tim turned the package over. "Might be." He went on eating his cornflakes.

Davy squinted at the packet. "MONSTER TYRANNOSAURUS REX!" it said. "GIANT DINOSAUR. EXTRA LARGE!"

"It *is* a T. rex!" Davy was breathless. "Can I see it? Can I borrow it? PLEASE?"

Tim finished his cornflakes with an irritating SLURP!

"No," he said, and he picked up the monster T. rex and stuffed it on the shelf above the fridge. "Gran sent it to *me*," and he went stamping off to get his football boots.

Davy gazed longingly at the shelf.

"Mum," he said, "do you think it would be OK if I had just a teeny tiny look at Tim's T. rex?"

Mum was rattling plates and bowls in the sink. "Better leave it where it is," she said. "You know Tim doesn't like you messing with his things. Wait until he gets back from school – he'll be more cheerful then."

"But do you think he'll lend it to me?" Davy asked. "Do you think he might?"

"Well . . ." Mum hesitated for a moment. "Perhaps."

"YES!" Davy punched the air. "It'll be the BEST thing in our display! He can sit on the very top of the mountain, and all the other dinosaurs will tremble!" And he hurried off to collect his homework and get ready for school.

Davy arrived in the classroom in a rush. He threw his coat at a peg, and dashed over to Mrs Frederick's desk.

"Mrs Frederick!" he puffed. "I've got EXACTLY the right thing to sit on the top of the mountain. It's a HUGE FANTASTIC AMAZING T. rex, and I'll bring it in tomorrow!"

"That sounds great, Davy," said Mrs Frederick, and she smiled. "I'll look forward to seeing it."

Davy zoomed over to his table, and whacked Sam on the back. "Just wait until you see my GIANT tyrannosaurus!" he boasted. "It's going to be the best thing in the display!"

Liam snorted. "Oh yes? So why didn't you bring it today?"

Davy hesitated for a millisecond. There was no way that he was going to say that the dinosaur wasn't exactly his yet. "I want it to be a surprise," he said.

Liam snorted again.

Davy ran all the way home that afternoon. He burst through the back door – but there was no sign of Tim. By the time Tim did finally reach home after football practice Davy was ready to burst. He had to hang on tightly to the kitchen table as Tim crashed through the door and dropped his football kit and muddy boots on the floor.

"TIM!" Mum said, but Davy was already there. "I'll take your boots outside!" he said. "And I'll clean them! And I'll polish them . . ."

Tim looked at Davy suspiciously. "What do you want?" he asked.

"I only want to borrow your tyrannosaurus rex," Davy said.

Tim looked blank for a moment, and then he grinned. "OK," he said. "Clean my boots and you can borrow it. Mr Prentiss says I'm playing for the under fourteens next week, and I'm going to be MUCH too busy to play with little kids' stuff."

"THANK YOU!" Davy shouted. "Oh, THANK YOU!"

Tim's grin got wider. "Hang on a moment. You can take my kit upstairs for me as well. And put it away – oh, but not my socks. They need washing."

Davy hesitated. Cleaning Tim's boots was one thing. Sorting out Tim's games kit was something else . . . but he really really needed T. rex.

He took a deep breath and nodded. "OK," he said, and he grabbed Tim's bag and rushed upstairs. His own bedroom was nearest, so he threw the muddy bag in through the door and slammed it shut. He'd sort it out later – just now he had far more important things to do.

Davy turned round, galloped back to the kitchen, thumped the boots on the mat and scraped at them furiously for half a minute with a stick.

"That'll do," he said, and he snatched the precious plastic package off the shelf.

"Hello, monster tyrannosaurus rex," he said happily as he pulled it out of its wrapper. "You're going to be the BEST!" And as Davy puffed and blew the folds of scaly plastic skin rippled, creaked, and swelled . . . and T. rex grew and grew and grew.

It was a wonderful looking beast.

It had amazing teeth that shone white in its huge and powerful jaws.

It had sharp claws that looked as if they were made of polished steel.

Its eyes were red and glaring, and as Davy puffed his last puff and carefully popped the little plastic stopper into place he heaved an enormous sigh of pleasure.

"Look!" he said to Mum. "Isn't it GREAT?"

Mum came to admire it. "Fantastic," she said, and then she looked a little closer. "Davy," she said, "I think it needs a bit more blowing."

Davy didn't answer. He was staring . . . and hoping and hoping that what he saw wasn't happening.

But it was.

T. rex was collapsing in front of him.

First the head sank, and then the body gave a hideously lifelike lurch. The lurch was followed by a stagger, and then another lurch . . . and finally total collapse.

Mum picked up the limp plastic shape and peered at it. "Oh no," she said. "There's a hole – see? There, in his foot. No – it's more like a little cut. Maybe Tim did it when he was opening the parcel this morning."

"Can we mend it?" Davy asked anxiously. "It's just GOT to be OK for tomorrow, Mum. Have we got some sticky tape or something?"

"We can try," Mum said, and when Davy went to bed that night T. rex was standing proudly on his bedside table. His foot was neatly criss-crossed with brown parcel tape.

"Is he OK?" Davy asked as Mum kissed him goodnight.

"He's fine," Mum said, and she laughed. "He looks like he's wearing a football boot." And she turned off the light. As she did so Davy remembered that Tim's football kit was underneath his bed.

"I'll take it downstairs in the morning," he thought sleepily.

Davy woke up in the darkness with his heart pounding.

Something had fallen on to his head – something smooth and soft and floppy. He pushed it away from his face . . . and then realized what it was.

"Oh NO," he groaned, and switched on his bedside light.

T. rex had collapsed again.

Davy sat up, his head in his hands, and thought of how Liam would laugh if T. rex collapsed at the top of the mountain. He imagined the huge dinosaur slowly folding up, crashing down the mountain slopes, and knocking over all the other dinosaurs as it fell. It would be terrible . . . whatever could he do? He punched his pillow angrily – and an idea flashed into his head.

"WOW!" he said, and hopped out of bed.

Davy's dinosaur was just as much of a success as he had hoped. It stood on the top of the mountain at the centre of the Dinosaur Day display, and everyone said it was brilliant. Liam and Ian giggled when they saw the sticky-taped feet, but Davy and Sam heaped sand over them, and nobody else seemed to notice.

Mrs Emms, the head teacher, was especially impressed. "It was very clever of you to think of stuffing him, Davy," she said. "I think that if he'd been filled with air he would have been too smooth looking. All those lumps and bumps in his back make him much more authentic."

Davy smiled happily, and tried his hardest not to yawn. It had been very late indeed by the time he'd finished pushing socks and T-shirts and shorts up T. rex's big back legs . . . but it had been worth it to see Liam's face when he'd carried T. rex in that morning.

He just hoped that Tim wouldn't need his football kit for a day or two.

THE DINOSAUR'S PACKED LUNCH

Jacqueline Wilson

Dinah doesn't feel like going to school. She crashes about in the kitchen getting breakfast and wakes her dad. He's cross, and now Dinah's cross, too – she has a fight with some boys at school and then she upsets her best friend. Grumpy Dinah thinks a school trip to the museum sounds boring, but she's in for a few surprises . . .

Dinah cheered up when they went into a special dinosaur exhibition. Dinosaurs were huge monsters who lived millions of years ago.

Dinah liked the look of dinosaurs.

Some of the dinosaurs were very fierce and vicious. Judy and Danielle squealed. Dinah didn't mind a bit.

The dinosaurs had huge long names to match their size.

Dinah wasn't very good at reading but she found she had no problem spelling out brontosaurus, and tyrannosaurus and triceratops.

She particularly liked the iguanodon. It had a funny pointed thumb spike. Perhaps the iguanodon sucked its thumb, too.

Miss Smith got cross because Dinah kept lagging behind.

"Hurry up, Dinah. It's lunchtime," said Miss Smith.

Everyone had a packed lunch except Dinah. Dad always forgot things like packed lunches. Sometimes Judy shared her packed lunch with Dinah. But not today.

"Ooh, my mum's given me prawn sandwiches and a bunch of grapes and a Kit Kat and a can of Coke. Want half my Kit Kat, Danielle?" said Judy.

Dinah crept away, feeling very empty. She wandered back to the iguanodon, sucking her thumb.

"I wish I had a mum to make me a packed lunch," said Dinah.

A hand reached out and patted her on the shoulder.

A huge scaly hand with a spiked thumb!

The iguanodon reached down and picked Dinah up. It cradled her in its arms, rocking backwards and forwards.

The iguanodon made Dinah her own packed lunch.

She ate a leaf sandwich, a bunch of daisies, a twig snack bar and a bottle of dinosaur juice.

The dinosaur juice was a very bright green. It tasted strange too, but Dinah drank a few drops.

The iguanodon wiped Dinah's mouth in a motherly way.

"Dinah! Where *are* you?"

Miss Smith was coming! Dinah jumped down and the iguanodon shot back into place with a rattle and a clunk. Miss Smith didn't see. She was cross with Dinah.

Dinah was too dazed to care.

All the other children were in the gift shop buying books and stickers and little rubber dinosaurs.

Dinah didn't have any money but she didn't mind. She didn't want a book or a sticker or a little rubber dinosaur.

She had just had a dinosaur's packed lunch!

Dinah was very quiet on the bus going back.

"You're not going to be sick, are you, Dinah?" Miss Smith asked anxiously.

Dinah wasn't sure. She felt very strange. She sucked her thumb, but it tasted strange, too.

She went to bed straight after supper. Perhaps she should have had a bath. Her skin felt strange now, hard and dry and itchy.

Dinah sucked her strange thumb and went to sleep. She dreamt very strange dreams.

When Dinah woke, something even stranger had happened.

She sat up and her head bumped against the ceiling! Her bed was so tiny she had to cram her knees right up under her chin.

Her bedroom had shrunk in the night.

No. Even stranger . . .

Dinah had grown. She had grown and grown and grown. She had grown a long back and long legs and a long tail!

Dinah gasped and sucked her thumb. At least she still *had* a thumb.

She wondered what to do.

She decided she'd better tell Dad.

She had to bend double to get out of her bedroom door and edge along the hall, her head neatly sweeping up the cobwebs (Dinah and her dad didn't bother about dusting) and then she had to bend right down again to get into Dad's bedroom.

"Dad. Dad! Wake up, Dad," said Dinah.

"What's the matter?" Dad mumbled. "Stop yelling at me, Dinah."

Dad peered out from under the bedcovers. He saw Dinah.

Dad was the one who did the yelling this time.

"Aaaaaaaaah!"

"A monster! A monster! Run, Dinah, there's a monster in my bedroom," Dad yelled.

"Hey, Dad. It's me, Dinah. I'm the monster," said Dinah. "Well, I think I've turned into a dinosaur, actually. It feels a bit scary. Give me a cuddle, Dad."

It was a bit scary for Dad, too. But he could see the huge dinosaur in his bedroom was wearing Dinah's nightie and talking with Dinah's voice.

It was his daughter Dinah all right. So he gave her a cuddle as best he could.

Then Dinah gave Dad a cuddle, which was much easier. It was fun being able to pick Dad up with her new arms. She'd have to remember to cut her claws though.

Her new skin didn't need a wash but her arms ached when she cleaned all her new teeth with Dad's big clothes brush.

Dinah was terribly greedy at breakfast. She ate a whole loaf of bread in one gollop and finished a jar of jam with one lick.

"Well, I'm a growing girl," said Dinah, giggling.

"I don't know how I'm going to afford to feed you now. Money doesn't grow on trees," said Dad.

Luckily, Dinah liked eating trees. Well, the leaves and the smaller snappier branches. And privet hedges taste delicious if you're a dinosaur.

Everyone got their hedges trimmed and their trees pruned for nothing.

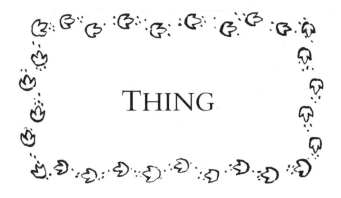

THING

Robin Klein

Emily Forbes and her mother lived in the top flat, and Mrs McIlvray, the owner, lived in the bottom one. Pets weren't allowed in the flats – it was a very strict rule. Mrs McIlvray always stared at Emily severely when they met on the stairs. She looked as though she suspected Emily of smuggling guinea pigs upstairs in her school-dress pocket.

Emily's mother was very understanding. She didn't say irritating things like, "Never mind, just pretend your nightie-bag pup is a real one." Or, "When you grow up you can have a farm with lots of animals." She said, "I just don't know how you can bear it, Emily! It's terrible! I just don't know how you can stand not having a pet!" Which made Emily feel noble and courageous.

It wasn't easy to look pleasant or interested when kids at school talked about their Labrador dog and how he could fetch the morning paper, or their grey Persian cat which let itself be worn as a neckscarf.

A gift shop near her school had pet rocks, with little plastic eyes glued on them, advertised for sale in the window. Having a rock for a pet seemed better than nothing at all. Emily didn't have fifty cents to buy one of the shop-window rocks, so she started inspecting the ground everywhere she went.

Rocks weren't plentiful in that suburb, and the huge ones in the park opposite the flats had been placed there by a crane. Emily knew she wouldn't be able to get one of those up the stairs by herself.

Then one day she found a beautiful rock. It wasn't anywhere special – the bulldozer working on the new sports oval near her school had scooped it up with a load of soil. Emily picked it up and rubbed it clean with the sleeve of her school jumper.

The rock was a cosy, rounded shape, and a gleaming, rich, dark brown, the colour of Vegemite in a new jar before anyone shoves a knife in to spread their toast. Emily took it home and put it on the living-room table, propping it up with a lemon squeezer because it was so smooth it tended to roll away.

"Mrs McIlvray couldn't possibly complain about your keeping a rock for a pet," said Emily's mother. "What are you going to call it?"

"I'll call it Thing," said Emily. "It's nice and short

and easy to remember." She patted the rock goodnight and went to bed.

Mrs Forbes, who was inclined to be vague about such matters, forgot to turn off the oil heater, and when they got up in the morning the living-room was like a sauna.

"Oh blah!" said Emily. "The heat cracked Thing."

"Rocks don't crack as easily as that," said her Mother. "Let me look." She picked it up and found that there *was* a crack, like an opening zip-fastener, and while she was looking it zipped open even more. The rock quivered in her hands, and made a peculiar slithery noise. Mrs Forbes made a louder one, and dropped it nervously on to the carpet.

Emily was more curious than alarmed, and she poked at the rock with the point of an HB pencil. Something inside tapped back, so she helpfully

tugged the two sections of the rock shell apart. A creature wriggled out, uncoiled itself and blinked at them. It was about half a metre long and a most attractive shade of green, like a Granny Smith apple.

"What on earth can it be?" asked Emily's mother. "I never saw anything like it before!"

"We did a project on dinosaurs at school," said Emily. "I think this could be a baby stegosaurus. They weren't as awful as those dinosaurs they have in horror movies, though. I think they were vegetarians."

"Oh," said Mrs Forbes, relieved. "You can give it that left-over coleslaw in the fridge, then."

"Come along, Thing," said Emily, and the little stegosaurus followed her into the kitchen. He ate the coleslaw, and four ripe bananas Mrs Forbes was saving to use for banana custard, and half a carton of mango yoghurt. While he was eating, he thumped his tail enthusiastically on the floor.

"If you keep him, you must tie newspapers round his tail to muffle the noise," said Mrs Forbes. "It's going to be difficult hiding him from Mrs McIlvray. I think they grow to quite a large size, Emily. Still, I suppose you can deal with each problem as it comes up."

The first problem for Emily was the worry about Thing being left on his own while she was at school and her mother was at work. Luckily she discovered that he liked television. While she was having her breakfast, she had the set switched on. Thing looked at it with great interest, then he jumped up on the couch and kneaded his little claws in and out of the couch cushions, making a contented purring noise. So Emily left the set turned on, with the sound very low.

When she came home from school, Thing was still on the couch, watching TV. He seemed to have grown a little during the day. Emily fed him a bunch of silverbeet which she had bought at the greengrocer's on the way home.

Mrs Forbes phoned from where she worked, as she did every day to make sure Emily got home safely.

"That stegosaurus should really be getting some outdoor exercise," she said. "I don't think dinosaurs just sat around watching TV in prehistoric times. You'll have to smuggle him out into the park, but don't let Mrs McIlvray see you both. And make sure no one notices you in the park, either, Emily. People can be very mean about animals being a nuisance. They're quite likely to whisk Thing off to a museum and put him in a glass box with a label."

Thing seemed to understand the need for quiet, even though he was so young. He padded softly after Emily down the stairs, and curled up his tail so that it wouldn't bump from one step to the next.

There weren't any people in the park, and Thing loved it there. He munched weeds and chased after autumn leaves, and rolled over for Emily to tickle his tummy. Then he sat down in the park fountain and gargled.

The only dangerous time was when a young man in a tracksuit went by, jogging. He blinked and slowed down. "Freeze, Thing!" whispered Emily, and Thing froze to look just the same as the rocks in the fountain, only mossier, so the young man jogged on.

When it was time to go back to the flat, Thing followed Emily obediently, and she got him

upstairs without being seen. But soon there was a knock on the door, and Mrs McIlvray stood outside, looking indignant.

"You've gone and brought a Saint Bernard dog in off the street!" she said. "The rule here, young lady, is NO PETS!"

"We don't have a Saint Bernard dog," Emily said truthfully.

"There are large muddy footprints on the steps, and they lead right up to this door!"

"Oh, they must be from my new plastic flippers," Emily said, not so truthfully. "I was testing them out in the park fountain. I'm sorry, and I'll wipe up the marks straight away."

"Kindly don't let it happen again," said Mrs McIlvray.

Emily didn't. She always took two pairs of old woollen socks and put them on Thing before she sneaked him back up the stairs after his daily ten minutes in the park.

Thing was really very little trouble. He spent all day watching television, with the tip of his tail in his mouth at the exciting bits. He didn't seem to mind what programmes were on. He liked them all: cartoons, classical music concerts, the news and weather forecasts, and even talks on gardening and cookery demonstrations.

At night he slept in a soft bed Emily made from a rubber inner tyre tube she got from the corner garage, and an old duffel coat she didn't wear anymore. Thing didn't care that it wasn't a nice, soggy, prehistoric marsh. He circled once or twice then settled down cosily with his nose resting on the tip of his tail.

He had a double row of bony plates down his back, and Emily kept them beautifully polished with Brasso. He grew to about the size of a small rhinoceros, and then stopped growing. Emily's mother was very relieved.

Thing liked living at Emily's place and being taken for walks. He became very clever at freezing into various shapes when necessary. He could make himself look like an ornamental fence, or a very large cactus on a nature strip. Emily was careful to take him for outings at times when there would be very few people about. The closest he came to being discovered was when they were out skateboarding early one Sunday morning.

They skated up and down the deserted shopping centre. Thing was too large and too heavy to ride the skateboard, of course, but he liked batting it along with his nose while Emily balanced on it.

A group of people from an adult landscape-painting class arrived to sketch the buildings. Thing hurriedly froze into a free-form sculpture in front of the council library, and Emily sat protectively on his tail and pretended to be adjusting the wheels on the skateboard.

"What an interesting sculpture!" said the artists, poking at him, and standing back with their heads on one side, looking most intelligent. "How very modern and unusual. And what marvellous texture the sculptor has managed to achieve with fibreglass!" Emily wished they would go away.

"It's not a free-form sculpture at all," said an elderly woman in a floral painting smock. "It's a young stegosaurus."

But nobody believed her, and Thing tried to stay frozen for a long time while the artists wandered all over the empty shopping centre practising how to sketch perspective. He was as stiff and creaky as a glacier when Emily was able to take him back to the flat.

"Never mind," said Emily. "We'll have a nice little game of kick-the-carton-the-groceries-came-in. Your goal is the couch, and mine's the kitchen door."

Thing was very good at that game, and he never cheated, either, although he had a tail he could have used, and Emily didn't. The game was very exciting, with five goals each, and they forgot to be quiet. Emily's mother was out, because she sometimes earned extra money at weekends driving taxis, so she wasn't there to remind them about Mrs McIlvray. Soon there was an angry knock on the door.

"Freeze, Thing!" whispered Emily, and he froze into the shape of a coffee table. Emily reluctantly opened the door.

"I'm sorry about the noise, Mrs McIlvray," she said. "I was practising ballet."

Mrs McIlvray looked past her into the living-room, which had become rather disarranged during the game of kick-the-carton. "I thought ballet was supposed to be pretty and graceful and quiet," she said frostily. "And that is a very odd coffee table you have there. Made out of green concrete, too. I don't think I can allow you to have concrete furniture in this flat. It might damage the floors." She came inside and peered critically at Thing, who had his head tucked under his stomach, and his tail tucked under to meet it. "It's not even very well designed, either," said Mrs McIlvray. "I should know, as I collect antique furniture, and I am an expert about good design. What are all those odd flaps sticking up on the surface? Most illogical, if you ask me!" She put on her reading glasses to examine Thing more closely, and tweaked the blades along his spine. She was very surprised when they moved.

"They're specially made like that," Emily said quickly. "They're to hold magazines and dried flower arrangements and cups of coffee."

"I really don't know how your mother could have bought such a frightful table," said Mrs McIlvray. "Just look at those heavy thick legs! They'll wear down the pile on my carpet. You must tell your mother that this thing has got to go back to wherever it came from!"

Thing heard, and was dreadfully upset. He remembered being in the rock egg at the sports oval, which hadn't been nearly as nice as Emily's place. He unfroze, whimpering, and scuttled over to Emily and hid his face in the front of her windcheater.

86

"It's a sort of mechanical table," Emily said desperately. "It can be used as a dish-trolley."

"You naughty little girl!" scolded Mrs McIlvray. "You know very well it's a nasty extinct animal of some kind! I'm certainly not having a dinosaur living in my block of flats! It belongs in a glass case in a museum. I'll give you until tomorrow night to arrange for its removal. And what's more, it has to stay out in the backyard while you're at school and your mother is at work. But it has to be gone by tomorrow evening!"

Emily felt so sad she could hardly bear it. Her mother, when she came home, went downstairs to plead with Mrs McIlvray, but it was useless. They gave Thing a wonderful feast of every vegetable and fruit they had in the kitchen, and let him stay up past midnight to watch the late night movie. But in the morning, Mrs McIlvray made them put him out in the back yard.

Emily went to school, crying so hard she had to pretend she had hay fever, and Thing stayed in the backyard. There was nothing happening there except leaves falling from Mrs McIlvray's maple tree, and he wondered why Emily hadn't brought down his TV set and plugged it in. He didn't like being in the yard very much. He chased after the drifting leaves, and played with the handle of the rotary clothes hoist.

Mrs McIlvray came out and scolded him sharply. She wound down the handle so tightly that it couldn't budge, and then she went out shopping. Thing looked wistfully over the front fence, but he knew he wasn't allowed to go out there without Emily to tell him when to freeze.

While Mrs McIlvray was away, a van was driven into the driveway of the flats, and two men got out. Thing quickly froze into something that looked like a length of pebbled patio. The men didn't knock at the door, or open it with a key. Instead, they pulled up the rubbish bin and stood on it and pushed in a flywire screen window to climb into the ground floor flat. Then they opened the door from the inside. After a while they came out carrying Mrs McIlvray's fur coat and her stereo record-player

and her new electric freezer. They put them into the van and went back inside the flats again.

They came out with Mrs McIlvray's antique oak writing-desk, which was extremely valuable, and her jewel box, and Emily's mother's electric sewing-machine. Thing was delighted to see the sewing-machine being taken away. Emily had to make an apron to pass a school craft examination, and she wasn't very good at sewing. She always looked glum while she was pinning on bias binding, and sewing it, and then unpicking it again because she had sewn it on back to front. Thing didn't like to see her look miserable.

The two men went inside and came out with Mrs McIlvray's antique jade and ivory statues and her nineteenth-century clock, and put them in the van. On their last trip of all they came out with Thing's TV set.

Thing wagged his tail, because he thought these men might kindly plug it in somewhere, and he could watch all the afternoon programmes instead of chasing maple leaves. But they put the TV set in the van with all the other items they had removed from Mrs McIlvray's flat and from Emily and her mother's flat. Then they shut the door of the van.

Thing unfroze a great deal more. He knew that his TV set contained cowboy movies, and Yoga five-minute exercises, and *How to Grow Better Roses*, and Fred Flintstone, and everything he liked to watch, and he wasn't going to let anyone take all that away.

He unfroze completely, went around behind the van, and tried to open the door with his nose. When that didn't work, he stretched out his neck and nudged the two men very politely.

One of them turned ivory and the other one turned jade, just like Mrs McIlvray's antique ornaments, and they leapt into the van and slammed the doors shut. They rolled up the windows at a tremendous speed, sealing themselves in like canned sardines.

They couldn't back their van out into the street, because Thing took up a great deal of space. He sat down and waited patiently for them to get out and unpack his TV set, so they just sat in the van and looked very upset and unhappy.

Thing was still sitting and waiting when Mrs McIlvray returned from shopping. At first she looked annoyed to see that he had got into her driveway, but then she noticed the broken flywire screen and the van crammed with all her valuable possessions. She dropped her basket and ran down the street to fetch the constable from the police station.

"We've been trying to catch those two burglars for months," the constable said. "They're a wicked, scheming, crafty, slippery pair of crooks. I'll take them down to the police station, and then I'll come back for the van. But would you kindly ask your dinosaur to step aside out of the way?"

The two burglars didn't look wicked or scheming when they had to step over Thing's tail and be taken down to the police station – they looked pale and worried.

Mrs McIlvray opened the van door and began to take her antiques inside, and Thing sat very quietly and humbly, with his tail tucked out of the way so he wouldn't be a nuisance.

But when Mrs McIlvray finished, she didn't look at him crossly — she bent down and patted him on the head.

"You needn't sit out in the draughty yard," she said, "you can wait in my flat until Emily gets home from school."

Thing wagged his tail and followed her inside, carrying his TV set in his mouth. Mrs McIlvray plugged it in and switched it on for him. He watched all his favourite afternoon shows, and when there was a demonstration on how to fold Origami paper into interesting shapes, Mrs McIlvray even cut up some bright gift-wrapping paper so he could practise. She kept telling him how grateful she was that he had saved all her precious belongings.

When Emily came home, still looking very hayfeverish, Thing was helping Mrs McIlvray unpack her shopping and stack it away in the right shelves. "I'm sorry he got out of the backyard," Emily said dolefully. "And I couldn't find any kid who'd give him a good home. Everyone's mothers said no they couldn't. No one seems to want a stegosaurus. I guess I'll just have to telephone the museum."

She couldn't bear to look at Thing. It was heartbreaking to think of your best friend permanently frozen in a labelled glass box. She looked instead at Mrs McIlvray, who was making a very expensive salad of broccoli and eggplant and avocado pear, decorated with little radish roses. Mrs McIlvray put the bowl of elegant salad on the floor in front of Thing.

"Museum?" she said indignantly. "What on earth are you talking about, Emily? If you don't mind my mentioning it, dear, this dinosaur of yours watches far too much television. It can't be very good for him. While you're at school during the day, I'll take him for a nice healthy run in the park – after we've had our lunch."

TOM AND THE DINOSAUR

Terry Jones

A small boy named Tom once noticed strange noises coming from the old woodshed that stood at the very bottom of his garden. One noise sounded a bit like his Great Aunt Nelly breathing through a megaphone. There was also a sort of scraping, rattling noise, which sounded a bit like someone rubbing several giant tiddlywinks together. There was also a rumbling sort of noise that could have been a very small volcano erupting in a pillarbox. There was also a sort of scratching noise – rather like a mouse the size of a rhinoceros trying not to frighten the cat.

Tom said to himself: "If I didn't know better, I'd say it all sounded exactly as if we had a dinosaur living in our woodshed."

So he climbed on to a crate, and looked through the woodshed window – and do you know what he saw?

"My hat!" exclaimed Tom. "It's a stegosaurus!"

He was pretty certain about it, and he also knew that although it looked ferocious, that particular dinosaur only ate plants. Nevertheless, just to be on the safe side, he ran to his room, and looked up "stegosaurus" in one of his books on dinosaurs.

"I knew I was right!" he said, when he found it. Then he read through the bit about it being a vegetarian, and checked the archaeological evidence for that. It seemed pretty convincing.

"I just hope they're right," muttered Tom to himself, as he unlocked the door of the woodshed. "I mean after sixty million years, it would be dead easy to mistake a vegetarian for a flesh-eating monster!"

He opened the door of the woodshed *very* cautiously, and peered in.

The stegosaurus certainly looked ferocious. It had great bony plates down its back, and vicious spikes on the end of its tail. On the other hand, it didn't look terribly well. Its head was resting on the floor, and a branch with strange leaves and red berries on it was sticking out of its mouth. The rumbling sound (like the volcano in the pillarbox) was coming from its stomach. Occasionally the stegosaurus burped and groaned slightly.

"It's got indigestion," said Tom to himself. "Poor thing!" And he stepped right in and patted the stegosaurus on the head.

This was a mistake.

The stegosaurus may have been just a plant-eater,

but it was also thirty feet long, and as soon as Tom touched it, it reared up on to its hind legs – taking most of the woodshed with it.

If the thing had looked pretty frightening when it was lying with its head on the floor, you can imagine how even more terrifying it was when it towered thirty feet above Tom.

"Don't be frightened!" said Tom to the stegosaurus. "I won't hurt you."

The stegosaurus gave a roar . . . well, actually it wasn't really a roar so much as an extremely loud bleat: "Baaa – baaa – baaa!" it roared, and fell back on all fours. Tom only just managed to jump out of the way in time, as half the woodshed came crashing down with it, and splintered into pieces around the stegosaurus. At the same time, the ground shook as the huge creature's head slumped back on to the floor.

Once again, Tom tried to pat it on the head. This time, the stegosaurus remained where it was, but one lizard-like eye stared at Tom rather hard, and its tummy gave another rumble.

"You must have eaten something that disagreed with you," said Tom, and he picked up the branch that had been in the dinosaur's mouth.

"I've never seen berries like that before," said Tom. The stegosaurus looked at the branch balefully.

"Is this what gave you tummy-ache?" asked Tom.

The stegosaurus turned away as Tom offered it the branch.

"You don't like it, do you?" said Tom. "I wonder what they taste like?"

As Tom examined the strange red berries, he thought to himself: "No one has tasted these berries for sixty million years . . . Probably no human being has *ever* tasted them."

Somehow the temptation to try one of the berries was overwhelming, but Tom told himself not to be so stupid. If they'd given a huge creature like the stegosaurus tummy-ache, they could well be deadly to a small animal like Tom. And yet . . . they looked so . . . *tempting* . . .

The stegosaurus gave a low groan and shifted its head so it could look at Tom.

"Well, I wonder how you'd get on with twentieth-century vegetables?" said Tom, pulling up one of his father's turnips. He proffered it to the dinosaur. But the stegosaurus turned its head away, and then – quite suddenly and for no apparent reason – it bit Tom's other hand.

"Ouch!" exclaimed Tom, and hit the stegosaurus on the nose with the turnip.

"Baaa!" roared the stegosaurus, and bit the turnip.

Finding a bit of turnip in its mouth, the stegosaurus started to chew it. Then suddenly it spat it all out.

"That's the trouble with you dinosaurs," said Tom. "You've got to learn to adapt . . . otherwise . . . "

Tom found himself looking at the strange red berries again.

"You see," Tom began again to the stegosaurus. "We human beings are ready to change our habits . . . that's why we're so successful . . . we'll try different foods . . . in fact . . . I wonder what fruit from sixty million years ago tastes like? Hey! Stop that!"

The stegosaurus was butting Tom's arm with its nose.

"You want to try something else?" asked Tom, and he pulled up a parsnip from the vegetable patch. But before he could get back to the stegosaurus, it had lumbered to its feet and started to munch away at his father's prize rose-bushes.

"Hey! Don't do that! My dad'll go crazy," shouted Tom. But the stegosaurus was making short work of the roses. And there was really nothing Tom could do about it.

He hit the stegosaurus on the leg, but it merely flicked its huge tail, and Tom was lucky to escape as the bony spikes on the end missed him by inches.

"That's a deadly tail you've got there!" exclaimed Tom, and he decided to keep a respectable distance between himself and the monster.

It was at that moment that Tom suddenly did the craziest thing he'd ever done in his life. He couldn't explain later why he'd done it. He just did. He shouldn't have done, but he did . . . He pulled off one of the strange red berries and popped it into his mouth.

Now this is something you must never ever do – if you don't know what the berries are – because some berries, like deadly nightshade, are *really* poisonous.

But Tom pulled off one of the sixty-million-year-old berries, and ate it. It was very bitter, and he was just about to spit it out, when he noticed something wasn't quite right . . .

The garden was turning round. Tom was standing perfectly still, but the garden . . . indeed, as far as he could see, the whole world . . . was turning around and around, slowly at first, and then faster and faster . . . until the whole world was spinning about him like a whirlwind − faster and faster and faster, and everything began to blur together. At the same time there was a roaring noise − as if all the sounds in the world had been jumbled up together − louder and faster and louder until there was a shriek! . . . And everything stopped. And Tom could once again see where he was . . . or, rather, where he wasn't . . . for the first thing he realized was that he was no longer standing in his back garden . . . or, if he was, he couldn't see the remains of the woodshed, nor his father's vegetable patch, nor his house. Nor could he see the stegosaurus.

There was a bubbling pool of hot mud where the rose-bushes should have been. And in place of the house there was a forest of the tallest trees Tom had ever seen. Over to his right, where the Joneses' laundry line had been hanging, there was a steaming jungle swamp.

But to Tom by far the most interesting thing was the thing he found himself standing in. It was a sort of crater scooped out of the ground, and it was ringed with a dozen or so odd-shaped eggs.

"My hat!" said Tom to himself. "I'm back in Jurassic times! 150 million years ago! And, by the look of it, I'm standing right in a dinosaur's nest!"

At that moment he heard an ear-splitting screech, and a huge lizard came running out of the forest on its hind legs. It was heading straight for Tom! Well, Tom didn't wait to ask what time of day it was – he just turned and fled. But once he was running, he realized it was hopeless. He had about as much chance of out-running the lizard creature as he had of teaching it Latin (which, as he didn't even speak it himself, was pretty unlikely).

Tom had run no more than a couple of paces by the time the creature had reached the nest. Tom shut his eyes. The next second he knew he would feel the creature's hooked claws around his neck. But he kept on running . . . and running . . . and nothing happened.

Eventually, Tom turned to see his pursuer had stopped at the nest and was busy with something.

"It's eating the eggs!" exclaimed Tom "It's an egg-eater . . . an oviraptor! I should have recognized it!"

But before he had a chance to kick himself, he felt his feet sinking beneath him, and an uncomfortably hot sensation ran up his legs. Tom looked down to see that he'd run into the bog.

"Help!" shouted Tom. But the oviraptor obviously knew as little English as it knew Latin, and Tom felt his legs sliding deeper into the bubbling mud.

Tom looked up, and saw what looked like flying lizards gliding stiffly overhead. He wished he could grab on to one of those long tails and pull himself up out of the bog, but – even as he thought it – his legs slid in up to the knee. And now he suddenly realized the mud was not just hot – it was *boiling* hot!

His only chance was to grab a nearby fern frond. With his last ounce of strength, Tom lunged for it and managed to grab the end. The fern was tougher and stronger than modern ferns, but it also stung his hand. But he put up with it, and slowly and painfully, inch by inch, he managed to claw his way up the fern frond until he finally managed to pull himself free of the bog.

"This isn't any place for me!" exclaimed Tom, and, at that moment, the sky grew red – as if some distant volcano were erupting.

"Oh dear!" said Tom. "How on earth do I get out of this?"

The moment he said it, however, he took it back, for the most wonderful thing happened. At least, it was wonderful for Tom, because he was particularly interested in these things.

He heard a terrible commotion in the forest. There was a crashing and roaring and twittering and bleating. A whole flock of pterodactyls flew up out of the trees with hideous screeching. The lizard creature stopped eating the eggs and turned to look.

From out of the middle of the forest came the most terrible roar that Tom had ever heard in his life. The ground shook. The lizard thing screamed, dropped the egg it was devouring and ran off as fast as it could. Then out of the forest came another dinosaur, followed by another and another and another. Big ones, small ones, some running on four legs, some on two. All looking terrified and screeching and howling.

Tom shinned up a nearby tree to keep out of the way.

"Those are ankylosaurs! Those are pterosaurs! Triceratops! Iguanadons! Oh! And look: a plateosaurus!"

Tom could scarcely believe his luck. "Imagine

seeing so many different kinds of dinosaur all at the same time!" he said to himself. "I wonder where they're going?"

But the words were scarcely out of his mouth before he found out.

CRASH! Tom nearly fell out of the tree. CRASH! The ground shook, as suddenly – out of the forest – there emerged the most terrible creature Tom had ever seen or was ever likely to see again.

"Crumbs!" said Tom. "I should have guessed! Tyrannosaurus rex! My favourite dinosaur!"

The monster stepped out into the clearing. It was bigger than a house, and it strode on two massive legs. Its vicious teeth glowed red in the flaming light from the sky.

The curious thing was that Tom seemed to forget all his fear. He was so overawed by the sight of the greatest of all dinosaurs that he felt everything else was insignificant – including himself.

The next moment, however, all his fear returned with a vengeance, for the tyrannosaurus rex stopped as it drew level with the tree in which Tom was hiding. Its great head loomed just above Tom and the tree, and made them both quiver like jelly.

Before Tom knew what was happening, he suddenly saw the tyrannosaurus reach out its foreclaws and pull the tree over towards itself. The next second, Tom found that the branch to which he was clinging had been ripped off the tree, and he was being hoisted forty feet above the ground in the claws of the tyrannosaurus rex!

Tom was too terrified to be frightened. A sort of calm hit him as the creature turned him over and sniffed him – as if uncertain as to whether or not Tom was edible.

"He's going to find out pretty soon!" exclaimed Tom, as he felt himself lifted up towards those terrible jaws.

"I bet," thought Tom, "I'm the only boy in my school ever to have been eaten by his own favourite dinosaur!"

He could feel the monster's breath on his skin. He could see the glittering eye looking at him. He could sense the jaws were just opening to tear him to pieces, when . . .

There was a dull thud.

The tyrannosaurus's head jerked upright, and it twisted round, and Tom felt himself falling through the air.

The branch broke his fall, and as he picked himself up, he saw that something huge had landed on the tyrannosaurus's back. The tyrannosaurus had leapt around in surprise and was now tearing and ripping at the thing that had landed on it.

And now, as Tom gathered his wits, he suddenly realized what it was that had apparently fallen out of nowhere on to the flesh-eating monster. I wonder if you can guess what it was? . . . It was Tom's old friend the stegosaurus – complete with bits of the garden woodshed still stuck in its armour plates, and the branch of red berries sticking out of its mouth.

"It must have given up eating my dad's roses and gone back to the berries!" exclaimed Tom. And, at that very moment, Tom could have kicked himself. "I'm an idiot!" he cried. For he suddenly noticed that the tree he'd climbed was none other than the very same magical tree – with its odd-shaped leaves and bright red berries.

But even as he reached out his hand to pick a berry that would send him back again in time, he found himself hurtling through the air, as the tyrannosaurus's tail struck him on the back.

"Baaa!" bleated the stegosaurus as the tyrannosaur clawed its side and blood poured on to the ground.

"Raaaa!" roared the tyrannosaur, as the stegosaurus thrashed it with the horny spikes on its tail.

The monsters reared up on their hind legs, and fought with tooth and bone and claw, and they swayed and teetered high above Tom's head, until the tyrannosaur lunged with its savage jaws, and ripped a huge piece of flesh from the stegosaurus's side. The stegosaurus began to topple . . . as if in slow motion . . . directly on to where Tom was crouching.

And Tom would most certainly have been crushed beneath the creature, had he not – at that very instant – found that in his hand he already had a broken spray of the red berries. And as the monster toppled over on to him, he popped a berry into his mouth and bit it.

Once again the world began to spin around him. The clashing dinosaurs, the forest, the bubbling mud swamp, the fiery sky – all whirled around him in a crescendo of noise and then . . . suddenly! . . . There he was back in his own garden. The Joneses' washing was still on the line. There was his house, and there was his father coming down the garden path towards him looking none too pleased.

"Dad!" yelled Tom. "You'll never guess what's just happened!"

Tom's father looked at the wrecked woodshed, and the dug-up vegetable patch and then he looked at his prize roses scattered all over the garden. Then he looked at Tom:

"No, my lad," he said, "I don't suppose I can. But I'll tell you this . . . It had better be a *very* good story!"

NOTE: If you're wondering why the magical tree with the bright red berries has never been heard of again, well, the stegosaurus landed on it and smashed it, and I'm afraid it was the only one of its kind.

Oh! What happened to the stegosaurus? Well, I'm happy to be able to tell you that it actually won its fight against the tyrannosaurus rex. It was, in fact, the only time a stegosaurus ever beat a tyrannosaur. This is mainly due to the fact that this particular tyrannosaur suddenly got a terrible feeling of *déjà-vu* and had to run off and find its mummy for reassurance (because it was only a young tyrannosaurus rex after all). So the stegosaurus went on to become the father of six healthy young stegosauruses or stegosauri, and Jurassic Tail-Thrashing Champion of what is now Surbiton!

THE MONSTER FROM UNDERGROUND

Gillian Cross

Bomber Wilson's class have been asked to write a Nature Diary, but Bomber hates writing and he can't think what to write about. Then he sees the road works. Bomber is fascinated by the ancient rocks the diggers are turning up and he decides to write about them. His neighbour Harriet thinks he's daft. Bomber is sick of her teasing, but then he has a brilliant idea — he won't write about the rocks, he'll do a survey of the night sky, so he can work at night when Harriet isn't around to laugh at him . . .

When his alarm went off at a quarter to twelve, he woke up and blinked. For a moment he couldn't think what was going on, because he had forgotten all about the survey of the night sky. And then, suddenly, he was wide awake.

Something had moved, just outside the window.

There was no shape to be seen. Just darkness. But the darkness had rippled and *moved*.

For a few seconds, Bomber was too frightened to breathe. Then the rippling happened again.

Very slowly, as if something was crawling past the window. On and on and on.

But it was an *upstairs* window! What was huge enough to block that? It would have to be bigger than an elephant!

Whatever it was, it wasn't looking in. Quietly he crawled out of bed and crept over to the window. Pressing his nose to the glass, he peered out at the stuff that was passing. It was rough and wrinkled, a bit like an elephant's skin. And where the moonlight caught it, he could see blotches and streaks.

Bomber's heart thudded with fright, but he wouldn't let himself run back to bed. Whatever the creature was, it was much too big to get into the room. It was worth trying to get a better look at it.

Carefully, Bomber pulled down the window catch. It squeaked a bit, but whatever was outside didn't take any notice. The skin just went on rippling past as he pushed the window open.

The smell nearly knocked him over.

It was like old grass cuttings and rotting plants, mixed with mushrooms and stale cabbage.

Bomber clapped his hand over his nose but, before he could recover, the door behind him was flung open. His mother appeared in her dressing gown, looking angry.

"Bernard, what *are* you doing? You woke me up from a deep sleep!"

Hadn't she noticed the smell? Bomber waved at the window. "Look!"

"At what?" said his mother.

Bomber turned back to the window, but there was no smell any more. No rough, blotchy skin. Just the dark sky, with the moon shining through the Newtons' apple tree.

The giant whatever-it-was had vanished.

His mother made him go to bed at once, but the moment she was out of the way, he switched on his bedside light. Very strange things were happening, and he wanted to make sure he remembered them. Grabbing his Nature Diary, he started to write.

> *I have just seen something very peculiar outside my window . . .*

On Thursday, Bomber made a plan.

He needed a witness.

Next time something strange happened, there had to be someone else there. Not one of his friends. Someone who wouldn't back him up unless he was telling the truth.

And he knew the ideal person.

At twenty to twelve that night, he was standing in the Newtons' back garden, throwing little stones up at Harriet's window to wake her up.

It worked brilliantly, because the window was open. Harriet stuck her head out, looking furious.

"*Bomber*? What's going on? That hit me on the nose."

"Sssh!" Bomber said. "Come down."

"Why? If you've touched my rain gauge —"

Bomber didn't bother to answer. He just backed away from the window and waited, staring up at the big, bright moon behind the apple tree. After a few minutes, Harriet crept through the back door.

"Are you crazy?" she hissed. "My dad'll go berserk if he catches you in our garden again. What do you want?"

"Wait a bit, and I'll show you," muttered Bomber. "And be quiet."

They waited. They stood with their backs to the house, staring down the hill. Far below, they could see the motorway road works but even those were still and quiet.

"It's funny," Harriet whispered. "Everything's very bright, but there's no moon."

"Yes there is," said Bomber. "Up behind the apple tree. It —"

And then he stopped. Because she was right. There wasn't a moon behind the apple tree, and there weren't any stars either. Instead, there was a big, black patch, as if something was standing between them and the sky. Something huge.

"Harriet —"

But before he could warn her, the black shape moved and they saw it properly. The monster. It had a vast, humped body and a long, thick neck that reared up into the sky. Its head looked ridiculously small as it peered over the top of the house.

Harriet gasped. She clutched at Bomber's arm and he clutched hers.

Slowly, the small head swayed from side to side, and they caught a whiff of the mushroomy, rotten-grass smell.

Then Harriet gulped. "Look at the apple tree!"

The creature's head bent down to grab at the top of the tree and the leaves shook, furiously.

When the head reared up again, there were black, leafy shapes sticking out of its mouth. A slow crunching, chomping sound came from somewhere up in the sky.

Bomber didn't dare to move, but he stared at the little head and the long, long neck. They reminded him of something. If only he could work out what . . .

And then – it vanished.

Suddenly, there was nothing there, except the big, white moon, behind the black branches of the apple tree. Harriet took a deep breath.

"What *was* it?"

"I don't know," said Bomber. "But I'm certainly going to find out."

When he got back to his bedroom, he wrote down all the details, underneath what he had written the day before.

> . . . *its body must have been six or seven metres high, and its neck reached even higher. It was a very long, thin neck, with a small head* . . .

He lay awake for hours, trying to think where he had seen a neck and a head like that. But his brain refused to work. He fell asleep at half past four, without having remembered.

But when he woke up the next morning, he *knew*.

He jumped out of bed and rummaged in the

bottom of his wardrobe. There was a great heap of polythene bags in there, full of old toys and games. Building bricks. Plastic aeroplanes. Model soldiers with their trucks and weapons. And somewhere ...

The bag he was looking for was right at the bottom. He tugged it out and emptied it on to the floor.

There were dozens of little plastic dinosaurs, all different shapes and colours. He shuffled through them, tossing away the stegosaurus and the tyrannosaurus, the parasaurolophus and the iguanadon.

And suddenly, there was the one he was looking for. He gazed at the long neck and the little head for a moment, and then turned it over to read the name underneath, to make sure he was right.

DIPLODOCUS.

Standing it on his bedside table, he sketched the shape carefully in his Nature Diary. Then he pushed it into his pocket. All the way to school, his fingers were curled round the thick body, feeling the long, long neck and the long, long tail.

Was it *possible?*

As he passed the road works, he stopped for a minute or two to look at the layers of rock in the cutting. The bottom layer was a long way down. It must be very old. And he could still see those strange lumps in it . . .

When he got to school, he didn't say anything to Harriet. He just took out the diplodocus and pushed it into her hand.

She stared. "But that's impossible. They've been extinct for millions of years."

"I know," Bomber said. "But look at it."

Harriet looked down at the dinosaur again. "Nobody will believe us," she said. "Unless we can prove it. How about a photograph?"

Bomber stared. Then, for the first time ever, he smiled at her. "Brilliant! Let's do it tonight."

They met in Harriet's back garden just before midnight, both carrying their cameras.

"We'll get better pictures if we're high up," muttered Harriet. "Because the creature's so big. Let's climb on to your shed."

They knelt on the roof, side by side, with the cameras held ready. At first they thought nothing was going to happen, but after ten minutes, Bomber nudged Harriet.

The apple tree was shaking. The fluttering leaves showed up clearly, with the full moon behind them. And then, slowly – very slowly – the huge black shape of the diplodocus began to move.

Bomber shivered. Suppose the monster saw them? Suppose it knocked the shed over? Suppose –

But it was no good thinking about that. If they wanted photographs, they had to stay there. He forced himself to hold the camera steady.

"Now!" hissed Harriet.

Both cameras flashed at once. The light was like an explosion, much brighter than Bomber had expected. It must have surprised the diplodocus too. Slowly, but not quite as slowly as before, it moved again – towards them.

Its head reared up, on top of its long neck, and began to sway from side to side, searching. Getting closer and closer. Harriet gulped.

"Let's get out of here!"

Bomber shook his head. "Wait. I don't think it'll hurt us. It's supposed to be a vegetarian." Crossing his fingers hard, he hoped all those scientists were right.

The head swayed closer and closer. It was small for such a huge animal – but it looked enormous as it came down towards them. Lower and lower it bent, until Bomber and Harriet were looking straight into its eyes.

The eyes of a dinosaur.

They were very pale, like pools of rainwater, and empty. Bomber stared deep into them. He couldn't tell whether the diplodocus saw them, but he was too scared to move.

Then Harriet grabbed his arm. "Photos!" she whispered. "We'll never get another chance like this."

Both together, they lifted their cameras. Bomber got the focus right and made sure the dinosaur's head was in the centre of his viewfinder. Then he said "Now!"

And the flashes went off together.

What happened then was mind-boggling. Bomber wrote it all down in his Nature Diary the next morning.

> ... *when the lights flashed, the dinosaur*
> *began to move towards us again. We couldn't*
> *escape, because it was too close. For one second,*
> *we could see it lurching forwards and then*
> *everything went dark and very strange. Tingling.*
> *The diplodocus walked right through us.*

Harriet got the photos developed on Saturday morning, and she took them straight round to Bomber's. When he opened the door, he could see that she was upset.

"What's the matter, Harry?"

"It's these. Look." She held out the photographs.

There were four beautiful pictures of the full moon behind the apple tree – but no sign of a dinosaur in any of them.

"There's nothing there," said Harriet. "Did we imagine it?"

Bomber shook his head. "I don't think so. Come down to the road works. I want to show you something."

They walked down together to the cutting in Hawthorn Hill and stared at the layers of rock. Like layers in a slice of cake – except that each one was older than the one above.

"The bottom layer must be very old indeed," Harriet said slowly.

Bomber nodded. "About a hundred and fifty million years."

"And those strange, enormous lumps?"

"Bones," said Bomber. "I reckon."

Harriet frowned. "Someone ought to have a look at them."

"I've been thinking about that," said Bomber. "I think I'll write to the local paper."

"Write? *You?*"

Harriet hooted with laughter, but Bomber just grinned.

Two weeks later, Bomber finished his Nature Diary. First, he pasted in the best of his newspaper cuttings. There was a large photograph of his face and underneath it said

SCHOOLBOY'S
DINOSAUR FIND

SCHOOLBOY Bernard Wilson has sharp eyes! He noticed some strange lumps in the excavations for the new M39, and wrote to his local paper about them. Now scientists believe that the lumps are the fossilized bones of a diplodocus – a huge dinosaur that has been extinct for millions of years.

There was a sketch of the diplodocus, too. The artist had got the face a bit wrong, and drawn the skin all scaly, but it was definitely the creature they had seen in Harriet's garden.

When he had stuck the cutting in, Bomber read through the whole diary again. He was amazed to see how much he had written. There was only one page left, and he knew what had to go on that. Picking up his pen, he began to write.

WHAT I'VE LEARNT

I'm sure we saw a diplodocus. Not a real one, because someone else would have noticed that. And a live diplodocus couldn't have walked through us.

I think it was a ghost. It started walking when its bones came to the surface in the road works. And it's stopped now the bones have been discovered.

I've thought a lot about this, Mrs Evans. Keeping an open mind, like you said. And I can't see any other explanation.

Mrs Evans was delighted with Bomber's diary.

Well done! she wrote underneath. It's crazy, but it's brilliant. And at last you've managed to write a *lot*!

And she gave him two gold stars and a special prize for the Most Original Entry.

She didn't say she believed Bomber's story, but she kept the newspaper cutting. And that afternoon, instead of lessons, the whole class went to see the dinosaur bones.

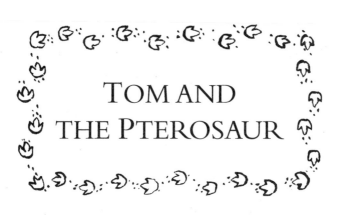

TOM AND THE PTEROSAUR

Jenny Nimmo

Mr Tuttle has been exploring the Amazon jungle, but now he is coming home and the family are looking forward to his return. Tom has some important news for him. While his sisters have been practising their carol singing, he has been investigating the weird sounds coming from his strangely secretive neighbours' barn, and made an amazing discovery – a real pterosaur, living next door!

Ten days after Mr Tuttle had left for his Amazon adventure, two postcards arrived from him. Mrs Tuttle's card had a picture of trees and monkeys on the front, the children's had a chameleon. The chameleon was quite hard to make out because it was almost the same colour as the branch it was sitting on.

On the back of the children's card Mr Tuttle had written:

There's so much I want to tell you, but it'll have to wait until I get back. It wouldn't all fit on this card. Children, I'm beginning to believe there are things in this world that no one will ever understand. I miss you all. Love from your dad xxxxxxxx

Those weren't at all the sort of words the dad Tom knew would have used. Mr Tuttle had always made it his business to understand *everything*. Tom wondered what had happened to his dad out there in the jungle.

Mrs Tuttle's card explained a bit more. "Your dad says he's met some Indians," she told the children, "and a medicine man who . . . who . . ." she brought the card closer to her nose and read it aloud, " 'who can summon up spirits. Audrey, I'm beginning to believe in the impossible. Me, of all people.' " Mrs Tuttle put the card down. "Well," she said. "Who'd have thought it?"

While Mr Tuttle was steaming in the jungle, his family was piling on blankets and muffling up in woolly hats and scarves. A hard white frost covered the fields, and even the trees were hung with icicles. Earth was indeed as hard as iron. And then the snow began to fall. Snow on snow.

Tom hadn't heard the pterosaur for over a week. He was uneasy. From his spyhole in the hedge he could see a deserted yard. The water trough was covered with a thick sheet of ice. A bucket had blown on to its side, the water inside it frozen solid. All the curtains in the Grimleys' house were drawn across. Could they have left home? And, if they had, what had become of their animals? Tom decided to find out.

Next morning he pleaded a sore throat. "I'b cubig dowd wib subthig, bub," he told his mother in a pretend coldy voice.

"You'd better stay indoors today," said Mrs Tuttle.

When the girls went to school, Tom was left behind, but he didn't intend to stay indoors. After breakfast he slipped a carrot and a tin of sardines into his pocket. Why the sardines? Tom would have said it was his sixth sense.

As soon as Mrs Tuttle started her washing machine, Tom put on his anorak, pulled on his wellies and stepped out into the icy air. CRUNCH! C R U N C H ! He plodded through the snow and out into the lane. The Grimleys' gate was rimed with frost.

Tom gasped as his fingers met the icy bars. He'd forgotten his gloves. He swung himself over the gate and thumped into the snow on the other side.

The yard was utterly silent. Mr Grimley's car, covered in snow, stood by the back door. There were no footprints, no tyre marks across the frozen yard.

Tom found Iris in the lean-to beside the barn. She brayed with delight when she saw Tom. "Hee-haw! Hee-haw! Hee-haw!" But the Grimleys' curtains didn't move.

Tom gave Iris the carrot and moved a bale of hay into her shelter. Then he took a spade and cracked the ice in the water trough. He filled a bucket with water and took it to Iris. By this time the chickens were calling from the henhouse. Tom found a sack of corn and scattered some of it on the floor. The ducks appeared to have flown away and the goats were happily nibbling things in the vegetable plot. There was only one thing left to do.

The bolts on the barn door were swollen with frost. Tom couldn't budge them. Again and again he blew on his freezing fingers, but his hands were numb with cold. He searched the yard and, beside a pile of logs, found a hammer.

CLANG! CLANG! CLANG! Tom hammered at the frozen bolts and, at last, they began to move. But the deafening blows made no impression on the Grimleys. Nothing stirred in the old house.

The second bolt slid back and the frozen door

shivered open. Tom stepped into the barn. He'd been too nervous to notice the smell before, but now it hit him. The fierce reek of stale air and muck. He opened the door wider to let in fresh air, and then, in the weak shaft of snowy light, he saw it — a dark shape right at the end of the barn. It was perched on a beam, its head drooping between folded wings. Its eyes were closed but the great spoon-shaped beak hung open and, as Tom approached, he could see the rows of treacherous teeth. There was no doubt about what it was. Birds didn't have teeth; their wings were feathery, not great sheets of skin.

"You're in a bad way, aren't you?" said Tom.

A rasping sigh came from the pterosaur.

It needed food and water. It needed sunshine

and hope. Tom could supply everything but the sunshine. He found an empty tin bath beside the door and carried it to the trough. When he'd filled the bath with water, he placed it close to the pterosaur's beam. Then he opened the tin of sardines and laid them beside the water.

The pterosaur didn't move. Tom stood as near as he dared and said, "I can't sing, but I'll tell you a story."

He stayed in the barn, talking softly until his voice had all but disappeared, and then he crept away. He didn't bolt the door, but left it open, just wide enough to let in a sunbeam, if any should appear.

Tom didn't tell anyone where he'd been or what he'd done. Not even Tabitha, who began to practise a new song as soon as she came home.

At teatime Mrs Tuttle suddenly slapped a hand to her head and declared, "It's Saturday tomorrow. I nearly forgot! Your dad's coming home. We'll all go shopping, shall we, to buy his favourite food?"

Tom wondered if he could slip a few tins of dog food into the trolley without anyone noticing.

That night the cold north wind did a sort of somersault and turned south. Tom lay awake, listening to the drip, drip of melting ice. In the morning the snow had thawed; it was rushing down the lane in a bubbling stream. The sun was shining and the world was green again.

Tom didn't have a chance to visit the pterosaur because he had to help clean the house and wash the car. At half past five Mrs Tuttle gave a yelp and said, "Quickly, everyone! Into the car. Your dad'll be home at seven. We've just got time to buy the feast."

The children piled uncomfortably into the Tuttles' ancient station wagon and, with groans and grumbles from the back, Mrs Tuttle drove rather dangerously to the supermarket.

They got there ten minutes before closing time. Only one checkout was open. The girl sitting behind it yawned and looked cross when the Tuttles came in.

"Won't be long!" Mrs Tuttle called sweetly. She grabbed a trolley and lifted Tilly into the little seat. Tamara took the list and began to throw things in. It was astonishing how quickly the trolley filled up. They raced round the aisles and managed to reach the grumpy checkout girl with a minute to spare.

"I hope I haven't forgotten anything," said Mrs Tuttle, pushing her trolley through the automatic doors. "It would be –"
Her voice came to an abrupt halt at the same time as her trolley.

The Tuttles stared into the car park, too amazed to speak.

There was something on top of their station wagon. Something huge. Its giant wings were folded like two tall umbrellas, and one of its talons appeared to have smashed the windscreen.

"A dinosaur," breathed Tilly.

"A *pterosaur*," said the twins.

"It can't be." Mrs Tuttle found her voice at last. "Pterosaurs are extinct."

"Not this one," said Tom. "It comes from next door." He didn't mention the sardines or the door that he'd purposely left open.

"I'll telephone the RSPCA," said Mrs Tuttle, swinging her trolley round. "Or the police – they'll know what to do. There's a phone in the store."

When she approached the automatic doors, however, they wouldn't open. The store was in darkness. Everyone had vanished. Even the car park was empty – except for the pterosaur.

Tulip began to cry and Tracy whined, "I'm starving. Can I have a biscuit?" She plunged her hand into the trolley, upsetting half its contents.

All at once the pterosaur shook its great wings. "AAAK! AAAK! AAAK!" it called.

Everyone screamed – except Tom.

"It's hungry," he said.

"Well, it's not having your dad's bacon," said Mrs Tuttle. "In fact, it's not having one tiny scrap of our welcome-home feast." And with that she swung her trolley round once more, and headed towards a shadowy gate that led to the back lane.

The children ran after her. "Mum, where are you going?" they cried.

"I'm going to push this trolley all the way home if I have to," panted Mrs Tuttle. "We can't use the car, that's for sure."

As they filed through the gate, Tom looked back. The pterosaur, craning its long neck, was watching them.

The lane was dark, but the lights from passing cars helped a little.

"It's miles," moaned Tracy. "All the frozen stuff will unfreeze."

"Let me push the trolley," said Tamara. "I can go faster."

"We'll take a short cut through the park," said Mrs Tuttle, handing over the trolley.

"If it's open," muttered Tamara.

Tom felt a tug on his sleeve. "You let it out, didn't you?" whispered Tabitha.

"Yes," Tom whispered, "but I didn't –"

"Why are you two whispering?" demanded Tamara.

"It's a secret," said Tabitha.

Mercifully the park gates were still open. The trolley bumped and squeaked as the Tuttle family pounded over the grass. They were halfway across the green when they felt the air stir and sigh and, looking up, they saw the two great sheets of the pterosaur's wings circling above them.

Everyone screamed again and Mrs Tuttle, forgetting all she'd said about Mr Tuttle's welcome-home feast, cried, "Leave the trolley and run, children. *Run!*"

"Where to?" they cried.

"The bandstand," said their mum. "At least we'll have a roof."

They raced towards the bandstand with its circle of lights under a pretty painted roof. Then they leapt up the wooden steps and crouched behind the railings.

"It's like a fairy's house," breathed Tulip through her sobs of fright.

They looked out to where the trolley stood in the thin gleam from the bandstand lights. And they gasped.

"Oh, children," cried Mrs Tuttle. "I forgot Tilly!"

There she was, her pale legs swinging from the trolley seat. The pterosaur had landed on a pile of tins at the other end of the trolley. It began to

peck at the packaging with its great beak. In a few seconds the dreadful spiked teeth would reach Tilly.

Mrs Tuttle was about to race across the grass, but Tamara and Tracy held her back. "You'll get eaten, Mum!" they yelled.

"Oh, what can we do? What can we do?" wailed Mrs Tuttle.

Almost without thinking, Tom said, "*Sing!*"

"Sing?" said Tamara, as though it were the silliest thing in the world.

"Yes, sing!" Tom repeated. "Singing calms it down. It makes it go kind of sleepy. If you all sing, then I can creep out and rescue Tilly."

"Can you?" Mrs Tuttle was too anxious to ask how Tom knew the creature's habits.

"What shall we sing?" asked Tabitha.

"The carol you sang when I was in the barn," said Tom. "You know, Tabs!"

Everyone looked at Tabitha. Tabitha opened her mouth but no sound came out.

"Come on! *Come on!* cried Tom. "Night and day you've all been singing, singing, singing. Surely you can manage a few tunes now!"

"Please *try*, girls," said Mrs Tuttle.

Tamara, Tracy, Tabitha and Tulip opened their mouths. What came out was a raggedy, frightened sort of moan.

"Do it properly," commanded Tom. "You've got

to start together, and keep the rhythm going." He began to tap the floor with his foot and, before he knew it, found that he was waving his arms about like Mrs Foley, the music teacher.

The girls stared at their brother in amazement. He was conducting. He was keeping time. He had rhythm.

"Tom, you *are* musical!" cried Tabitha.

"Musical boys don't always sing," murmured Mrs Tuttle.

"Girls, concentrate!" said Tom.

They all began to sing.

When the Tuttle Band was singing smoothly, Tom looked over his shoulder. The pterosaur had turned towards the bandstand. Its eyes held a mysterious gleam. No sound came from Tilly. She was gazing intently at the huge creature.

Tom thought, She's not afraid of dinosaurs. She thinks she knows them, because of all the stories I told her. He wondered if he could be as brave as Tilly, and shivered, wishing that he didn't have to run out into the darkness all alone.

"I'm going now," he said. "Keep up the singing."

"I'll come with you," whispered Tabitha. "It'll need two of us."

"OK." Tom grabbed his sister's hand and together they crept down the steps and out on to the shadowy grass.

The pterosaur was motionless. It stared at the

bandstand, its gaze never wavering as the twins tiptoed behind it.

"Don't make a sound," Tom whispered to Tilly. "I'm going to lift you out of the trolley."

Without a word, Tilly put her hands on Tom's shoulders. Her eyes were wide and shining. Tom heaved and Tabitha pushed Tilly's feet. Tilly wriggled until she was out of the seat and clinging to Tom's neck. Tom glanced at the pterosaur. It looked like a statue, it was so eerily still. The girls' voices rang out in the cold air.

"The world in solemn stillness lay
To hear the angels sing."

What could that sound mean to an ancient creature? Tom wondered. "Let's go," he whispered.

The twins ran towards the fairy lights. When they had almost reached the bandstand, Mrs Tuttle swooped over to them and gathered Tilly into her arms.

"I'm so sorry," she cried. "I forgot you, Tilly!"

"It's only a dinosaur," said Tilly.

"A *ptero*saur," panted Tom.

The sudden burst of activity had broken the spell. The pterosaur turned away from the singers and began to tear at the packages in the trolley. Out tumbled the sausages, the bacon and several chops.

"There won't be any food left," whined Tracy.

But all at once the great creature stopped eating. Was it sorry that the singing had ended? Whatever it was, the pterosaur decided to abandon the trolley. Spreading its wings, it sailed into the distant shadows.

"Where's it gone?" said Tamara.

"I don't care," said Mrs Tuttle. "I'm going to get that trolley."

"You're joking!" cried Tracy.

Mrs Tuttle wasn't joking. "I've forgotten too many things today," she said, "but I'm not forgetting your dad's feast – what's left of it."

Down the steps she bounded, and out into the dark and dangerous spaces of the park. Seizing her trolley, she ran, ran, ran across the grass while the children raced behind her, Tamara carrying Tilly piggyback. They didn't stop until they reached the gate on to the main road, and even when they were safe on the pavement they kept on running.

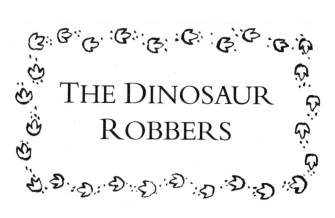

THE DINOSAUR ROBBERS

Jeremy Strong

The trouble with Max was that he looked just like his Dad. They both had wild tufts of ginger hair that seemed to explode from their heads. They both had big spectacles that magnified their eyes. They both looked like mad inventors.

Actually Max's Dad *was* a mad inventor, so that was OK. But Max just got teased by the Grabbly Gang at school. There were three of them, all brothers, and all bigger than he was. They called him Mad Max, or Fish-Tank, because his eyes seemed to swim behind his glasses. They knew it made him furious and once he even shouted back at them.

"I'll get my big brother onto you!"

The boys burst out laughing. "You haven't got a big brother! Honestly Max, you're as crazy as your Dad!" And they began to chant. "Max is dotty! Max is potty! Max has spots upon his botty!"

Max wanted to get back at the gang but, of course, they were bigger than he was. He wished he *did* have a big brother. All his friends had big brothers, and they seemed to be very good at sorting things out. He glared at the Grabbly Gang from a safe distance. There was quite a lot of sorting out he would like to do to them.

One day Max came home from school and found his father looking even madder than usual. As soon as Max appeared his Dad came leaping up the path and pounced on him. "Max – come and see!" he shouted, and pulled Max into the back garden. "There! What do you think of THEM?"

Max goggled. His eyebrows went right up and his jaw went right down. Standing in their little garden were two life-sized, shining metal dinosaurs. One had three very pointy horns and powerful, fat legs, as thick as tree-trunks. "This is my friend Triceratops," said Max's Dad, "and this is his big brother, Tyrannosaurus Rex!" Dad stood underneath the huge monster and peered out from between its legs. High above him the massive jaws were open wide. Its razor-teeth glinted in the sunlight. And then – Tyrannosaurus moved.

Max screamed as the mighty metal meat-eater snapped its jaws with a loud CLANG of metal teeth. His heart tried to leap out of his body and run away all by itself. His eyes bulged so much they almost smashed out through his spectacles.

"It's OK," grinned Dad. He reached into the open belly of the beast. "I just press this button and everything stops." The gruesome giant ground to a halt. Max sat down and waited for his heart to stop sounding like ten raving rock-drummers all playing at once. His father seemed very pleased with himself. He stood there with all his hair standing up like an astonished porcupine. "I've made these for a museum display. Come and look inside."

Dad lifted Max up so that he could peer inside. The robot was full of motors and cogs and wheels and chains. "There's the STOP-START button. Those levers make it go right or left," explained Dad. "The big motor drives the legs. It's the same with the triceratops. Pretty good, aren't they? Tell me I'm very clever . . ."

"You're very clever," Max admitted. "Can I have a go?"

"I thought you'd never ask. You can be Tyrannosaurus and I shall be Triceratops. Shall we dance?" They climbed inside the two creatures and it wasn't long before the dinosaurs were waltzing round the garden, like two monster ballet-dancers from a strange dream.

It was all great fun, but there was one big problem. Max and his Dad were blissfully unaware that they were being sneakily watched by a very sneaky pair of eyes.

Binbag had the sneakiest eyes in the street. He and his wife Buster lived just round the corner from Max. Buster and Binbag were robbers. Nobody knew they were robbers of course, because they

were very cunning. Buster had arms like a JCB, with lots of tattoos down them. She got her name from busting into houses. Binbag was very thin and scrawny. After his wife had smashed into a house he would nip inside and stuff all the valuables into black bin-bags, and that was how he got *his* name.

Binbag leaned out of his bedroom window. He stared at the dancing dinosaurs in Max's back garden. "Whoopee!" he cried. "See those robot dinosaurs? Guess what? We're going to steal one!"

"What do you want a robot dinosaur for?" demanded Buster. "You big baby!"

"We shall use it to break into the jewellery store on the High Street," said Binbag.

"Brilliant idea!" shouted Buster. "Have a smackeroo!" And she gave her husband a big, wet kiss.

That same night the robbers crept into Max's garden. Buster sat on top of Triceratops and Binbag climbed inside. He pushed the STOP-START button and grabbed the levers. Triceratops lurched into action and they went galloping off down the road.

Buster and Binbag made straight for the jewellery store. They aimed their three-horned battering-ram at the super-duper-triple-strength window and charged towards it at top speed. "Yee-hah!" yelled Buster. "Ride 'im cowboy!"

KER-LUMP, KER-LUMP, KER-LUMP, KERRACKETTY SMASH!

Glass went everywhere. Binbag dashed inside the battered building and stuffed fistfuls of jewels into a black sack.

"Tally-ho!" cried Buster, and the robbers jumped back on to Triceratops and went galumphing back to Max's home. They parked Triceratops in the garden. Then, just as if nothing had happened, they took their sack of jewels and went off home, whistling all the way.

The daring robbery made front page headlines. The police couldn't work out how the thieves had managed to break that extra-tough window. The only clue they had were several gigantic footprints, unlike anything they had seen before.

The *Daily Times* carried a photograph of the mysterious footprints. Over breakfast Max stared at it for a long time. He gazed out at the silent metal dinosaurs standing in the garden. "Do those footprints remind you of anything?" he asked his mother, who was busily pouring milk on to her husband's cereal and singing "One milk bottle slopping in the bowl . . ."

"Yes. We haven't got anything for supper."

Max wrinkled his nose. "Why do they remind you that we haven't got any supper?"

"Because they are the same size as empty dinner plates."

Max groaned and turned to his father, but Max's dad was too busy stirring his soggy cereal and thinking of a way to make it crisp.

Max sighed and set off for school, still staring at the paper. He knew that the photograph was some kind of clue. He took care to avoid going past the Grabbly Gang's house, but they saw him all the same.

"Look," they laughed. "Max is going to solve the mystery of the jewel robbery. Watch out everyone – Detective-Inspector Fish-Tank is hot on the trail!" Max was beginning to think that a machine-gun would be even better than a big brother.

By the time he went to bed he still hadn't got to the bottom of the puzzle. He slept badly, dreaming about dinosaurs wearing enormous spectacles and ballet frocks. At half past two his troubled sleep was broken by strange noises from the garden.

Max woke with a start. He pulled on his glasses and peeped out of the open window. Two shadowy figures were creeping round Triceratops. Buster grinned at his wife. "Triceratops makes a brilliant battering ram! That jewellery store was a piece of cake," he boasted. Max almost fell out of the window. Of course – those footprints had come from Triceratops! The jewellery thieves had used Dad's Triceratops!

"What a very nice man to make us these lovely monsters to play with," giggled Buster. "What shall we rob next?"

"Let's go for the big one and break down the bank. Ten-tonne Tessie will smash down the bank's walls in no time at all."

"Ooh, lovely!" cried Buster. "What a jolly idea! Have a smackeroo!"

"Gerroff," gasped Binbag. "We've work to do." He gave his wife a leg-up on to the beast's broad back, climbed inside and Triceratops went clumping off down the road.

Max was in a frenzy. What on earth was he to do? He rushed into his parents' bedroom. "Mum! Dad! Robbers! Robbers have taken Triceratops and they're going to rob the bank!"

"Doobee-doobee-dah!" squawked Max's mother sleepily, dreaming she was the lead singer in a rock band.

"Dad! Wake up!" panicked Max, pulling at his father's arm.

"Urra-urra," snored Dad. "Soggy cereal . . . yukk! I shall invent milk that isn't wet. That's it! I shall invent crisp milk!" And he carried on inventing in his dreams.

This was terrible! Max hurtled downstairs and out into the garden. He had to stop those robbers. Max plunged into the garden shed and pulled out his bike. He leaped on to it, and immediately remembered that he had a puncture. His heart sank. He threw the bike to the ground and stared down the dark road in despair.

Max would have to rouse his parents. He began to run across the garden, and immediately fell flat on his face. He had just tripped over Tyrannosaurus's left foot. Max stared up at the roaring monster. Moonlight glinted on the long teeth.

And that was when it happened, like a sudden shooting star. KAPPOWWW! Max had an incredible idea. He dashed to the kitchen, grabbed a chair and stumbled back outside. He stood on it, pushed open the door in the beast's belly and climbed inside.

Max punched the STOP-START button and the motors began to hum. He pushed a lever and the jaws snapped shut with a clang. Whoops – wrong one! Max tried not to panic. He had to remember the right levers. He made another attempt.

Tyrannosaurus lurched forward and began to march across the garden. Max could see the garden fence straight ahead, but this was no time to stop and politely open the gate.

KERRUNCH! Tyrannosaurus crashed through the wooden fence and set off down the road with bits of broken planking clinging to its sides. Max calmed himself. He was in control now and he headed straight for the bank in the High Street.

Tyrannosaurus broke into a bone-jarring trot. There were red traffic lights ahead. Max held his breath and plunged straight through them, right across the path of a cruising police car. Whoops again! Max gulped hard as the night air was shattered by the scream of a siren. The police car raced up alongside the galloping dinosaur, its blue light flashing eerily. Max went even faster. The police driver was so busy goggling at the dinosaur that he drove straight into a litter-bin with a shuddering KER-THUDD! Paper, empty cans, apple cores, banana skins and old crisp packets erupted into the air and came splattering down on the car.

Outside the bank Triceratops stamped his enormous feet. He lowered his heavy three-horned head and lumbered towards the door of the bank.

KERLUMP KERLUMP KERLUMP KERRASH!

"Do it again!" ordered Buster, and Triceratops smashed into the door once more.

KERRASH-KERRUNCH! The thick wood began to splinter.

"It's almost done!" Buster cried.

For a third time Triceratops's full weight crashed head-first into the door. It burst from its hinges with an ear-splitting crack and toppled to the floor. Binbag jumped out of the beast. He looked deeply shocked. "Oh dear," he said. "Look what we've done. We've smashed down the door. Aren't we naughty?"

"*Aren't* we naughty!" giggled Buster. "Have a big smackeroo!" And she gave Buster the biggest, wettest, slurpiest kiss ever.

"We shall be millionaires!" grinned Binbag.

"We shall be *squillionaires!*" Buster shouted, giving Triceratops a bone-crushing hug. Binbag grabbed a sack.

"Come on, you daft carrot! Leave that dinosaur alone. We've got a bank to – Eeek!"

Binbag could only point and gawk, for round the corner came a gigantic rip-roaring, jaw-crunching, fist-punching, teeth-flashing, burglar-bashing tyrannosaurus rex.

Tyrannosaurus Max came thundering up the

High Street, just as Buster and Binbag struggled madly to climb onto Triceratops and make their escape. The monster screeched to a halt and loomed over the two robbers. "Run for it!" squeaked Binbag, but it was too late. High above them Tyrannosaurus's huge jaws yawned open and a thunderous voice boomed out.

"There is no escape!" Max's voice echoed and boomed along the dinosaur's long metal throat and out of the gaping mouth.

"Who are you?" trembled Buster. "We've done nothing. We were just going to take out a bit of pocket money ..."

"Liars!" roared Tyrannosaurus Max. "Cheats! Robbers! Have a smackeroo!"

With a sweep of his massive head he knocked Triceratops on to its side. Four fat legs paddled away uselessly in mid-air. Buster fell in a rain puddle and Binbag scrambled to escape from inside, but it was quite pointless. Max reached down with his short front arms and grabbed them both. Buster and Binbag twisted and wriggled like a pair of freshly caught fish. Max set off at once for the police station.

Inside the police station a dazed police constable was trying to tell his sergeant that he had almost driven into a tyrannosaurus rex, but had crashed his car into a litter-bin instead. "I really did see a tyrannosaurus!" cried the policeman. "As tall as a house!"

"Yeah, yeah," muttered the sergeant, "and I'm Mickey Mouse." Just then there was an almighty roar from outside. The sergeant rushed out and found himself face to face with a tyrannosaurus rex dangling Buster and Binbag in front of his nose. The door in the belly opened and Max jumped out.

"Hello," he grinned at the goggle-eyed sergeant. "I've brought you these two thieves. I caught them up the High Street, robbing the bank." And he explained all about Triceratops and the jewellery robbery.

Buster and Binbag very quickly found themselves behind bars. Meanwhile, Max climbed back inside the tyrannosaurus and headed towards home. However, he made a little detour on the way.

The tyrannosaurus stopped outside a house that Max knew only too well and usually tried to avoid at all costs. Max knew just which bedroom the Grabbly Gang would be in, and their window was open. How very useful!

Tyrannosaurus Max squeezed his iron-fanged head through the window. The metal mega-monster tapped one of the Grabbly Gang on the head with a sharp claw, then poked and shook the other two boys. All three of them woke and sat up, wondering what was going on. And then they saw.

"Aaaaaargh! There's a tyrannosaurus in our bedroom! Aaaaaaaaaaargh! Tyrannosaurus Attack! We're all going to die! Aaaaaaaaaaargh!" The Grabbly boys vanished screaming beneath their covers, like jibbly-jobbly jellies, whilst the tyrannosaurus opened its gigantic jaws and roared.

"Do you know who I am?" bellowed Tyrannosaurus Max.

"Don't eat us!" screeched the three boys.

"I'm Max's big brother. Any more trouble from you three and I *will* eat you – is that understood? I shall gobble you up like kebabs!" And with that Max gave an enormous burp. He poked all three boys once again just because it felt so good, pulled his head out of the bedroom and clomped off down the road, giggling.

Max parked the tyrannosaurus in his own back garden and wearily climbed up the stairs to bed. He peeped into his parents' room, but they were still fast asleep. "Crispy, crunchy milk . . . yum-yum!" muttered Max's Dad.

"Tra-la-la whaaaa!" trilled Max's Mum, who had now left the rock band and was deep into opera.

Max smiled and shut their door. He crawled into bed and lay there for a moment, thinking. Mad Max? Never! Fish-Tank? No way! Tyrannosaurus Max? That would do nicely. He closed his eyes and drifted into a contented, dreamless sleep.

Acknowledgements

The publisher would like to thank the copyright holders for permission to reproduce the following copyright material:

Tony Bradman: The Agency (London) Ltd. for "Dilly's Pet" by Tony Bradman, first published by Piccadilly Press 1989. Copyright © Tony Bradman 1989. **Lindsay Camp:** the author for *Dinosaurs at the Supermarket* by Lindsay Camp, Viking 1993. Copyright © Lindsay Camp 1992. **Gillian Cross:** Egmont Children's Books Ltd. for extract from *The Monster from Underground* by Gillian Cross, Heinemann Educational Books 1990. Copyright © Gillian Cross 1990. **Terrance Dicks:** Penguin Books Ltd. for "The Littlest Dinosaur" from *The Littlest Dinosaur* by Terrance Dicks, Hamish Hamilton 1993. Copyright © Terrance Dicks 1993. **Vivian French:** the author for "Davy's Dinosaur" by Vivian French. Copyright © Vivian French 2002. **Terry Jones:** Pavilion Books, a division of Chrysalis Books Plc. for "Tom and the Dinosaur" from *Fairy Tales* by Terry Jones. Copyright © Terry Jones 1992. **Dick King-Smith:** AP Watt Ltd. on behalf of Fox Busters Ltd. for "Use Your Brains" from *A Narrow Squeak and Other Stories* by Dick King-Smith, Viking 1993. Copyright © Fox Busters Ltd. 1993. **Robin Klein:** Curtis Brown (Aust) Pty Ltd. on behalf of the copyright owner, Robin Klein, for *Thing* by Robin Klein, Oxford University Press 1982. Copyright © Robin Klein 1982. **Margaret Mahy:** The Orion Publishing Group Ltd. for "The Strange Egg" by Margaret Mahy from *The First Margaret Mahy Story Book* by Margaret Mahy, J. M. Dent Children's Books. Copyright © Margaret Mahy 1972. **Jenny Nimmo:** Walker Books Ltd., London, for extract from *Tom and the Pterosaur* by Jenny Nimmo, Walker Books 2001. Copyright © Jenny Nimmo 2001. **Jeremy Strong:** David Higham Associates Ltd. for *The Dinosaur Robbers* by Jeremy Strong, Macdonald Young Books 1996. Copyright © Jeremy Strong 1996. **Jacqueline Wilson:** The Random House Group Ltd. for extract from *The Dinosaur's Packed Lunch* by Jacqueline Wilson, published by Doubleday. Copyright © Jacqueline Wilson 1995.

Every effort has been made to obtain permission to reproduce copyright material but there may be cases where we have been unable to trace a copyright holder. The publisher will be happy to correct any omissions in future printings.

Titles in the
Kingfisher Treasury series

~